Independence

By

Laura Hesse

Believe in miracles

Other books by Laura Hesse

The Holiday Series:

One Frosty Christmas
The Great Pumpkin Ride
A Filly Called Easter
Independence
Valentino

Childrens Stories:

Gus
The Flood
The Unicorn King
The Unicorn & The Dragon
The King of Christmas

Adult Fiction:

The Thin Line of Reason
Gumboots

Non-Fiction:

Peter Pan Wears Steel Toes

To find out more about Laura Hesse or be the first to read a preview of Laura's next release, visit www.RunningLProductions.com

Laura Hesse

Independence

COPYRIGHT© 2006 Laura Hesse

All rights reserved. No part of this publication may be reproduced or transmitted in any form or by any means or stored in a database or retrieval system without prior written permission of the publisher.

The author and the publisher make no representation, express or implied, with regard to the accuracy of the information contained in this book. The material is provided for entertainment purposes and the references are intended to be supportive to the intent of the story. The author and the publisher are not responsible for any action taken based on the information provided in this book.

All characters in this publication, other than those clearly in the public domain, are fictitious and any resemblance to real persons, living or dead, is purely coincidental.

National Library of Canada Cataloguing in Publication Data
Hesse, Laura - 1959
Independence/by Laura Hesse
Previously titled, Two Independents/By Laura Hesse

ISBN 10 digit: 1539002284
ISBN 13 digit: 978-1539002284

CIP:**I. Title. PS8565.E84553T86 2006**   C813'.6   C2006-902135-X

Cover Design: Shardel

Distributed Worldwide by Amazon

Publisher
Running L Productions
Vancouver Island, British Columbia, Canada

Website: www.RunningLProductions.com

Independence

Acknowledgments

It takes numerous professionals to finalize the production of any publication and heartfelt thanks go out to my editor, Dianne Andrews, and my beta reader, Sharon Meadows.

The biggest acknowledgment, however, must go to Don Brown and Yvonne Olson and their wonderful team of Fjords, without whom, this book may not have been written. Yvonne and her "kids" were most patient with this cowgirl during her first attempts at driving a team.

My thanks,

Laura L. Hesse

Contents

California or Bust 1

CD 7

The Sale 17

Susie 29

Susie's Big Night Out 37

Company's Coming 47

The Cattle Drive 61

Stetler's Pond 84

Better than Birthdays 97

On the Hunt 108

Summer's Inferno 115

The Great Escape 134

Love's Rhapsody 147

Appendix: Picture of a basic driving harness 158

Valentino - a preview 160

Independence

Laura Hesse

Prologue

California or Bust

The sun blazed in the sky. Sun-worshippers walked along the beach, lovers strolled hand-in-hand, and children playfully galloped in front of their parents. They looked like carnival goers in a House of Mirrors, their tanned bodies shimmering in the heat waves that hung over the sand. Many others stretched out on towels, their bodies lathered with sunscreen, their skin beaded with sweat.

A beach umbrella flew into the air and went crashing across the beach, its owner racing after it, as a sudden gust of wind blew in across the ocean.

It was a typical summer day on Venice beach in California.

Sun glistened off of the ocean. Whitecaps of spray barreled overtop of the rolling waves as the wind began to whip up the waves ever higher.

It was what the surfers had been waiting for. They grabbed their boards and ran for the waves, taking advantage of the incoming tide and the five to six foot

Independence

swells that began to pummel the beach.

Among the surfers were two teenage boys and a girl. The boys were lean and tanned, one with pimples and unruly black hair that fell over his eyes like a sheepdog, the other was blond and cherub faced. The girl was lithe and athletic, her long blond dread-locked hair tied back to reveal sparkling blue eyes. The three laughed and ran into the surf, tossing their boards ahead of them, and then diving onto the slick surfaces to skim across the waves.

They paddled out, boards bucking and tossing against the ever-increasing height of the surf. They spun round in one expert move and paddled hard, arm muscles stretching taught. Expertly, they stood up and rolled forward, riding the pulse of the ocean waves, darting left and right to avoid a collision with each other, broad smiles across their faces as they rode into shore.

As soon as they hit the shallows, they raced back into the surf, laughing.

The girl glowed. She raised her face to the sun and smiled as she paddled effortlessly back out to sea.

A large black Freightliner truck with a large sleeping cab in the back and shiny chrome grills in the front pulled into the parking lot above the beach. Grey exhaust billowed from its twin chrome exhaust pipes that rose like silver chimneys behind the sleeping cab. It pulled into a loading zone and parked. Red and yellow four way hazard lights started blinking on and off. The driver stepped out of the cool air-conditioned cab and into the scorching summer sun.

The man wore a plain black t-shirt, faded jeans, and cowboy boots. Wild blond hair and piercing blue eyes peeked out from beneath a Toronto Blue Jays baseball cap. He stuck out like a sore thumb as he walked across the beach towards where the three teens were surfing.

"Susie!" Thomas Stetler yelled over the crashing of the waves and roar of the wind.

Out on the surf, Susie and the boys sat on their surfboards, legs dangling in the water, the waves rolling the boards up and down. Susie turned, shading her eyes as she looked towards the shore. She frowned.

"Who's that geek?" Mark, the raven haired boy, asked.

"Check out the boots," the angel-faced Simon said.

The boys laughed. Susie remained mute.

"Susie!" Thomas waved to her. He then motioned her to come in to shore.

Reluctantly, Susie caught the next wave in and surfed expertly in to the beach. The boys shrugged at each other and followed after her.

Thomas smiled and walked across the beach towards her. Susie hoisted up her board and carried it across the sand. He tried to help her, but she pulled away.

The boys jumped off their boards and quickly picked them up, racing after their friend.

Susie stopped by the teens' pile of towels. She dropped her board, picked up a towel, and began to dry herself off. More than one young man on the beach eyed the beautiful girl as she did so, wishing that he had the courage to approach her, and more than one girlfriend glared balefully at her, but Susie was oblivious to them all.

"Nice boards," Thomas commented to the boys.

"If you're looking for lessons, you'll have to catch up with Scud," Mark returned.

"Scud?"

"Yeah, he runs the board shop beside the pier," Mark answered. He pushed his hair back to get a better view of Thomas. There was something familiar about him, but

Mark couldn't quite figure out what it was. "He's ex-Delta Force or something, but he's alright."

"Hence, the name 'Scud'." Thomas grinned. "Thanks, but I'm not here for lessons."

"Good thing, dude, the boots ain't kosher," Simon joked.

"Kosher, too funny," Mark fist-bumped Simon.

Susie finished drying herself off, through her towel over one shoulder, and then wordlessly picked up her surfboard.

"See you guys," she said, walking away.

"Hey, Sus, where you going?" Mark called.

"Yeah, what's up?" Simon echoed, confused.

Susie waved a hand over her head and kept walking, heading towards the waiting truck.

"Nice to meet you, boys," Thomas said, tipping his ball cap to them. He then dashed after his daughter, his cowboy boots sinking deep into the sand.

"What just happened, Markie-Mark?"

"Dunno," Mark replied.

"You didn't have to embarrass me," Susie said to her father as they reached the parking lot.

"How'd I embarrass you?"

Susie didn't answer.

Thomas sighed.

They reached the truck.

Susie watched Thomas climb up on the running boards and unlock the doors. He then reached in and started rummaging around in the cab.

"Where are we going to put my board?"

"I got that covered," Thomas said, holding up a couple of orange nylon straps and a black nylon bag. "Here, zip your board into this so it doesn't get scratched. We'll tie it on to the frame behind the cab. It'll be safe and sound back there."

Her father's thoughtfulness almost made her cry. Susie knew she should say something nice, but her whole world was crashing down around her, so she simply took the offered surfboard cover from his hands and focused on covering her board.

Outside of the small pink two bedroom stucco bungalow with palm trees in the lane and a chipped clay Koi fish spewing dirty water into a dust coated fountain beside the front door, Susie and her mother fought bitterly. A knapsack was slung over Susie's shoulder and a battered leather suitcase rested on the ground at her feet.

Her father waited patiently inside the cab of the air conditioned truck.

"I don't want to go to B.C.!" Susie shouted.

"I'm tired of fighting with you, Susie," Susie's mother, Sharon, shouted back, one hand slicing through the air to punctuate her statement, her shoulder length straight black hair bobbing up and down.

"It's because of Wally, isn't it? He's the real reason you're shipping me off!"

"No, it's you! I've had enough, Susie. I'm tired of fighting and I'm tired of your lies."

"I'm not the liar, mom!"

Sharon lifted her hand, about to slap her daughter across the face, but stopped in mid-strike. She took a step backwards, horrified at herself.

"I think everyone needs to cool off," Thomas yelled as he jumped out of the truck and rushed over to where his ex-wife and daughter continued to argue. "It's time to go,

Susie. Let's not have the cops escort us to the state line."

Thomas picked Susie's suitcase up off the ground, but she tore it out of his hands.

"Just make sure Wally doesn't sell my board while I'm gone," Susie warned her mother as she stomped off.

"You see what I'm dealing with? Now you understand why I need a break? It's your turn. I'm done," Sharon fumed.

Thomas raised his hands, palms up, trying to soothe her.

"Chill out, Sharon. Take a deep breath. Susie will be fine. I'm sure she'll love being back at her grandparents farm."

"Good luck with that."

Sharon spun on her heel and stormed into the house, slamming the door shut without even a backwards glance.

"Good grief," Thomas muttered, tipping his hat back.

Behind him, he heard the door to his truck slam shut.

He turned around and walked slowly back to the truck. His daughter glowered in the passenger seat, her jaw taught, eyes blazing with fury.

"He's going to sell my board," Susie growled at her father as he slipped into the driver's seat beside her.

"You don't know that."

"Yes, I do."

"I'm sure Wally isn't that nasty."

"You don't know him. Wally can make a Great White Shark look like a guppy."

Thomas sighed in defeat, placed the truck in gear, and pulled away. He had the feeling it was going to a long drive.

Chapter One

CD

The large, brawny Norwegian Fjord gelding stood solemnly in the middle of the pasture, giant head cast downwards, thick black and white mane hiding a wide neck, the pupils beneath his closed eyelids moving restlessly. His coat was the color of creamy butter. At thirty years of age, he was still a handsome horse, but there was something about his stance and his manner that nagged the soul and tugged at the heartstrings.

June Stetler sat on the porch soaking up the sun and watching her old horse dreaming. Her Irish wolfhound lay at her feet, his long, lean body stretched out across the floor boards, his wiry hair ruffled by a gentle early summer breeze, his grizzled face brushing the tip of one loafer. She could feel his breath, as faint as a puff of smoke, on the exposed skin between her sock and her pant leg. Her two wooden canes rested against the low cedar table beside her, the curved hand-rests smooth and worn.

June suspected she knew what her gelding, CD, was dreaming about and felt the tears threatening to flow once again. Chester, CD's companion of twenty years, had passed away three months ago.

The big Fjord had suddenly become a tired old man, his once proud gaits now slow and plodding, his eyes grown dull, and his coat had lost some of its luster. Heartbreak crippled him. Those that thought that horses had no feelings didn't know them very well and had never seen one grieve.

June picked up her cup of tea and took a sip. What to do, she wondered. Something had to be done for poor CD. Her daughter-in-law, Melissa, drove over each day to check on the gelding and to report on his condition to her husband, Thomas. Thomas was a long distance truck driver; he was on the road most of the year. Thomas was only five years old when the wobbly young colt was born. The colt arrived on Canada Day, July 1st, at five a.m. in the morning. Thomas named the foal, Canada, thinking that was most original. It got shortened to CD fairly quickly.

June grinned. CD soon proved that he had been aptly named. The young colt was stubborn, independent, fiercely loyal, and most tolerant of the five-year-old boy who doted on him, crawled beneath his legs, and in general, made himself a positive nuisance.

June cast a glance at the low mountain that shadowed the skyline in the distance. She could just make out the meandering road that her husband had cut for her fifteen years earlier when arthritis had first begun to cripple her hips and bend her back. Prior to that, it had been a lovely forest trail, the track thin and meandering, just wide enough for a rider and a packhorse to fit through, but then a custom built wagon had replaced the western saddle and packs so the cathedral like trail had been widened.

The horses didn't seem to mind. The sound of jingling harness being lifted off the hook in the barn made CD and Chester eager to be off. They would prance up the mountain, the wind lifting their thick manes, their muscles rippling as the wagon bounced its way up the winding path to the alpine meadow where a tiny log cabin nestled amidst the wild flowers on the borders of a cool spring fed lake. The horses loved it. June never had to worry about tying them; neither wanted to go home, and neither did she.

"Penny for your thoughts," Bill whispered, pushing open the screen door and stepping out onto the porch. The dog opened his eyes and wagged his tail; it thumped like a sledgehammer against the porch's wooden floor. Bill reached down and patted the dog's head. The wolfhound yawned.

June smiled sadly.

"I was just wondering what to with CD," she confessed.

Bill sat down on the chair beside her. He sighed wearily. He wasn't a horseman. Like his son, he drove big rigs for a living and was gone most of the time. The horses kept his wife company and he was grateful for the happiness they brought her, but dealing with a heartsick horse was out of his realm.

"Well," Bill consoled her, "he's not all alone. He does have the sheep."

The wolfhound lifted his head and let out a low rumble.

"Oh, sorry, Horse. Yes, he has you too." Bill scratched one of the giant dog's ears. The wolfhound's tail thumped harder.

June chortled in amusement.

"I don't think Ruffles and Moppet are quite the same as Chester. Horse, of course, is another story, aren't you, boy?"

The dog pushed himself up lazily, stretched and leaned his lanky frame against June. The wolfhound stood more than three feet at the shoulder. He turned his bright eyes toward her and looked down at the top of her head.

"No, I suppose they're not," Bill replied, pushing the dog away. "Rather short, I'd say."

"Hmmm, and a little wooly," June countered.

"Right smelly too, they are," Bill finished. "Can't stand the little beggars myself so I suppose I can't blame CD for not wanting to be bothered either."

Horse let out a low woof.

"We're not talking about you. You're family. We're discussing the sheep, dear." June chuckled and glanced sideways at her husband. "You are a bit daft sometimes."

"Are you talking to me or the dog?" Bill asked his wife.

"You!"

"Aye. I suppose I am when it comes to horses and sheep," Bill agreed.

June laughed. Horse groaned, licked June's hand and thumped back down onto the porch.

CD heard the couple talking and looked up. He swung his head around so that he could see them with his good eye, his right being completely blind, and let out a short whinny.

"Now, you've done it. You've woke him up," June chided her husband.

"Ah, well, it's time he got up anyway, it's almost noon," Bill winked.

"Help me up, dear," she said, picking up her canes and leaning forward in the chair.

Bill placed a hand under his wife's elbow and helped her to her feet. She gripped her canes, one in each hand, steadying herself, and carefully stepped down to the ground. Horse followed along obediently behind her, being careful not to knock either of the canes. CD nickered a greeting, louder than the first, and started walking toward the fence.

"Right, love. We're coming. You know I don't move that fast anymore," June said to the gelding.

Bill wandered across the yard beside his wife of forty years, his lips pursed, his brow furrowed.

They reached the split-railed fence and waited for the gelding to arrive. The two sheep bleated and trotted up beside the Fjord, obviously expecting a treat.

"Here comes Dewey and Louie," Bill groaned.

"Now, now, dear. I know you aren't fond of them, but Melissa loves them," his wife said.

"Well, then she can take them home with her," he said grumpily. "I'd be delighted to pop the pair of them into the backseat of her Buick. I'm sure they'll fit. Once you get past all that hair, they're really quite thin."

"I thought they were supposed to keep CD company," June teased her husband. "And it's wool, not hair."

"Humph," Bill grunted, not impressed.

The gelding slipped his head over the fence and cuddled up to June. He nuzzled Bill's sleeve and accepted a gentle pat. He snorted and licked his lips, pleased to have some attention. The sheep tried to push him aside, but CD wasn't so inclined. He nipped Moppet's soft, wet nose and the sheep jumped backwards out of the way. Horse growled a warning as Ruffles tried to butt her way in.

"Good boys, keep those sheep at bbaaaay," Bill cheered, stroking both the horse's thickly corded neck and the dog's wiry head. The wolfhound's back was almost level with the horses'.

CD snorted and hung his head over Bill's shoulder, and then playfully nibbled on one of the wolfhound's ears. The dog looked up at the horse with trusting eyes, his lips almost curling into a smile.

"For a man that knows nothing about animals, you do have a way with them."

Bill laughed. "Ah, CD and Horse just know who supplies the bread and butter."

June grinned, her spirits lifting.

The couple stood close to the old Fjord, cooing and fussing over him until his dark mood lifted. The sheep lost interest and wandered away to graze. The dog lay down and dozed in the afternoon sun.

"Sam Morrison called this morning and told me there's a horse sale over at Jim Wiseman's. I think we should go. CD obviously has good taste and won't hang out with sheep so let's go find him a new buddy," Bill said, squaring his shoulders.

The wolfhound looked up and tilted his head sideways.

"Don't look at me like that. You don't count. You live in the house, much to my objections, since you're as big as a horse too. CD needs someone outside. I don't expect you're willing to give up the couch, are you?"

Drool dripped from the dog's mouth.

"I didn't think so."

"I don't know, Bill. CD's thirty! I don't think I can handle a young horse anymore and I expect that's all that will be there. I doubt that CD will even take to another horse."

"Nonsense! CD's got lots of life left in him and maybe a youngster is what he needs. That or we'll find him a pony pal."

"You've been thinking about this for some time, haven't you?" June said, raising an eyebrow.

"Only for a couple of days and you can blame Sam Morrison and your daughter-in-law for that! It was Melissa's idea. By the way, she's coming with us," Bill confessed.

June howled with laughter. Her long red hair, graying gently at the temples, bounced off her shoulders. The sun glistened off the copper tresses. Her gray eyes sparkled with life. She reached out and tugged her husband's blue ball cap down over his eyes. He grinned and flipped it backwards so that it hung on his head at a jaunty angle.

"You are such a devil, and so is Melissa. No wonder our Thomas married her, she's just like you," June said with a shake of her head.

CD nipped Bill's arm playfully.

"See? CD wants a new buddy, don't you?"

The gelding lifted his head and shook himself fiercely. A wave of dust rolled off him like a plume of ash erupting from a volcano. It clogged the air and choked the lungs. Horse sneezed.

"There! I am right. CD agrees completely," Bill said proudly, wrinkling up his nose and waving a hand in front of his face to keep the dust from his eyes.

"He was just shaking the flies off, dear." June chuckled.

A car drove into the lane and pulled up beside the house. A tall, auburn-haired woman climbed out of the car at the same time as a wiry eight-year-old, freckled-faced boy jumped out of the passenger side and slammed the door shut. He grinned, and then bolted towards his grandparents. He was a boy who didn't do anything in slow motion.

The sheep bleated loudly and ran for cover, galloping off across the pasture as if a mountain lion was on their tails. CD whinnied, a spark of blue fire blazing in his one good eye. He snorted and banged a leg against the fence, his mane bouncing against his neck. The old gelding loved the little boy.

"CD!" young Billy Stetler screeched happily, skidding to a stop in front of his grandparents and the dun-colored Fjord. "Horse!" he shouted at the dog.

"Billy!" his mother gasped. "How many times do I have to tell you not to run up to horses like that? One day, you're gonna do that to the wrong horse."

"Awe, CD won't hurt me and neither would Chester, if he was still here," the boy scowled. The dog looked the boy straight in the eye, and then licked the top of his head. "Aw, Horse, yer giving me cooties."

The gelding too brushed his nose across the top of the boy's head, ruffling the curly locks, and then began to nibble on a strand of copper-colored hair. Billy tried to push both the dog and the horse away, but they only ignored him.

"CD's getting old, Billy, and lots of horses don't like little boys," Melissa replied, and then broke into a grin. She knew it was a lost cause. Billy didn't listen to her any better than she had listened to her own mother when she was that age. Her mother always said that one day she would get her revenge, and then along came Billy. All in all, she considered herself lucky; Billy was a good kid. He was mildly wild, but had a heart as big as Canada itself.

"Come on, CD, I brought you a carrot so stop chewing on me," Billy thumped the gelding on the neck and pulled a carrot out of his back pocket. He offered it to the horse. CD dropped the strand of hair he was munching on and nipped the end off the carrot. The wolfhound let out a low woof and licked his lips.

"Yeah, I got a biscuit for you too," Billy said, pulling a treat from his other pocket. The dog accepted it gently and crunched the biscuit in two, his tail thumping crazily.

"So, you ready, mum?" Melissa asked.

"Was this *your* idea?"

"Not all together," Melissa said, looking sheepish.

"Oooh, I can see why your mother thinks that you deserve that boy of yours." June laughed, her eyes shining as she beamed down at her grandson. Billy looked over his shoulder and grinned at his grandmother.

"She sure does," he agreed.

Everyone laughed.

"Well, I see I'm outnumbered, but I'm not going to agree to bring a horse home with us," June warned her family, "or a pony pal either." She fixed her husband with a steely look.

"That's fine. We're only going to look anyway," her husband nodded.

"Yeah, right," Billy said, giving CD a final pat. "Horse, you gotta stay here. You're too big for the car."

June gave Billy a gentle slap on the rear end. Billy giggled. The four bid the Fjord and the dog a farewell and headed out to the horse sale, leaving the animals to stare after Melissa's blue Buick as it disappeared down the road. The gelding turned around and walked back to the spot where he had been dozing earlier, closed his eyes, and let his shoulder muscles droop. Birds chirped. Crickets chirruped. The noise lulled him into a peaceful sleep. The dog watched the horse settle down, and then lowered his head between his paws and closed his eyes.

Chapter Two

The Sale

Melissa drove up the bumpy road that led to the Wiseman's ranch and pulled the Buick into a makeshift parking lot in the field in front of a large steel equipment shed. The lot was full to overflowing. There were very few cars. Most of the vehicles parked there were three-quarter ton trucks with stock trailers attached. Fuzzy noses poked out of the slats in many of the trailers, the horses inside waiting their time to enter the auction ring.

The heavy equipment usually stored in the large shed, including plows, tractors and backhoes, stood in a line in an outlying pasture. Instead of equipment, there were horses of all shapes and colors, from deep chestnut to dark bay, from multicolored paints to spotted Appaloosas, tethered inside the shed. Makeshift stalls had been thrown together; old gates and sheets of plywood were fastened into large box stalls, both outside and inside of the main barn.

The auction was a big one. A number of the larger ranches had brought down their unwanted stock in the hopes of finding them good homes.

The auctioneer's voice boomed over a loud speaker as several cowboys put their reining mounts through their paces in the riding ring. A large Stetson clad crowd urged them on. Cow horses spun on their haunches, hooves digging down deep, as the rider brought out the best in each one. There was lots of applause and nodding of heads.

"Five hundred! Who'll give me five hundred for the little chestnut with Brad Smith aboard? This little gelding comes from the Circle K Bar, out of good working stock folks. He'll cut cows 'til he drops. Look at that boy cut! He's a bargain at any price," the loud speaker blared. The cowboy astride the small reining horse dipped him first right, and then left, the gelding's hind end tucking in tight as he ducked back and forth, chasing an imaginary cow.

A hand went up in the crowd.

"Five hundred! Who'll give me five-fifty?" the auctioneer yelled.

And so it went. The auction had begun.

"Wow, look at that fella move," gasped Billy. "Mom, can I have a horse like that?"

"Not on your life," his mother gawked. "I had no idea that a horse could move that fast."

Bill and June chuckled as the four of them approached the sales ring.

"That's 'cause you're a city girl," Bill winked.

"And you aren't?" June chided her husband.

"Grandma, grandpa's not a girl!" Billy chirped.

"You're right, Billy, he's not, but he is a city boy."

"Did you used to ride like that, Grandma?" Billy asked, his eyes wide with wonder, as the cowboy snaked a rope around one of the bystanders and backed the gelding up until the rope was taut and the helpless bystander had to wait until he was let go. The crowd crowed with laughter.

"When I was your age, I did, but not anymore." June tousled her grandson's hair.

"See! I'm not too young, mom. If grandma could do it, so can I," Billy announced. He pursed his lips and folded his arms across his chest.

"Well, if you want to ride like that then you better find a cowboy who's willing to teach you because your grandma isn't up to it and your mother doesn't know how," Bill scolded him gently.

Billy screwed up his face and thought hard for a moment.

"Okay, I can do that," he said and bolted off into the crowd.

"Oh, heaven help us," Melissa sighed.

A series of loud laughs erupted from the men leaning against the fence rails, studying the new set of horses that were just being ridden into the ring. One of them waved at the auctioneer.

"It seems we have a young man here today who's looking for a cow horse and a cowboy to teach him how to ride it. Any takers?" the auctioneer asked.

There was a chorus of cheers as a good-hearted rancher lifted Billy up to sit on the fence so that everyone could see him. Billy waved, a huge smile on his face, his gray eyes twinkling; sure that someone would help him.

Sam Morrison, the Stetlers immediate neighbor, stepped up and yelled over the commotion.

"Well, I guess that we might have a horse at home that'll do, but you're gonna have to work for it, young man. I expect you to help drive our cattle up to summer pasture the same as every other cowboy that works for me," Sam offered amiably.

"Okay!" Billy shouted. "Do I get to wear a hat?"

The men all around him slapped their legs and howled with laughter.

"I reckon," Sam Morrison said, in a serious voice. "There ain't no such thing as a cowboy without a hat."

The men clustered around Billy nodded in agreement.

"Hey, Mom!" Billy shouted. "I'm gonna be a cowboy afore you know it."

"Oh, Lord, what is his father going to say?" Melissa paled.

"Don't worry about that," Bill placed a reassuring hand on her shoulder. "Thomas used to work for Sam in the summer too. He was about Billy's age when he started."

June smothered a laugh, her eyes tearing up with the effort of holding it back. She finally gave up and let loose with a hearty belly laugh, having to lean heavily against her canes to keep from toppling over.

"I wonder if Sam still has that old Appaloosa?"

"Wouldn't surprise me," Bill said.

From over by the ring, Sam looked around for the Stetlers, saw them, and tipped his hat to Bill and June. He nodded at Melissa; the laugh lines around his eyes deepening with mirth.

"Well, I'm glad we came, for young Billy's sake, but I don't think that we're going to find a horse to replace

Chester with at this auction. The horses here are all ranch-bred Quarter horses," June said, looking around.

Billy ran back to his mother and skidded to a stop, almost knocking her to the ground. He was breathless, his cheeks a candy-apple red.

"That is so cool. I'm gonna learn how to rope cows too, Mr. Morrison promised," he gushed.

"I hope you shook his hand to seal the deal?" Bill nudged his grandson.

"Yep, sure did," Billy said smartly.

"Then you make sure that you don't embarrass the family and learn what he has to teach you."

"Yes, sir," Billy advised his grandfather.

June guffawed. Melissa kept silent, still not sure how she was going to tell her husband about this.

"Well, young William, how about you accompany your old granny to the barn and we'll see what else there might be for sale in there," June offered.

"Neato," Billy said, sidling up beside his grandmother.

"You're supposed to tell me that I'm not an old granny," June teased her grandson.

Billy looked up at her and smirked. "Okay," he said, and then dashed away.

The three older Stetlers giggled, turned and walked slowly toward the large red barn. Bill looped his arm under Melissa's and tugged her forward. Melissa shook her head, realizing that it was her own fault that her son now wanted to be a cowboy since it really had been her idea to bring June to the auction in the first place.

The noonday sun beat down on the old barn's tin roof making it as hot as a giant skillet. Heat waves shimmered outside, but inside the barn was a cool oasis. Horses nibbled peacefully inside their stalls, their faces half buried in timothy, ignoring the people that poked and prodded at them through the steel railed stalls. Others were more fearful, range bred and skittish, working horses used to being left alone until they were needed. Some stuck their noses through the bars and nuzzled at passing pockets, hoping for a treat.

Bill, June, Melissa, and Billy, wandered by each of the stalls and looked the horses over. They stopped to pat a few of the more social ones. Bill and Melissa quickly realized that June was right; the likelihood of finding a companion for CD was indeed very slim. Content, they ambled through the barn together, commenting on one horse or another, simply enjoying the time the family was spending together.

"How about that cute pony over there, mum?" Melissa pointed at an old black pony standing quietly to one side eating a pile of hay as if it was his last meal on earth.

"No, I don't really want a pony," June replied.

"Who'd ride it?" Billy asked, eyeballing his mother. He wasn't dumb; he knew what she was thinking.

"Well, you could exercise him for your grandmother," Melissa offered.

"I don't think so! Cowboys don't ride ponies," Billy groaned.

Bill and June exchanged a look and smiled. Melissa's motives were all too clear. They had tried the same thing on Thomas; it hadn't worked then either.

In the far corner of one aisle, they came across a string of fancy Tennessee Walkers, their bodies sleek and graceful, their heads elongated. At the end of the string was a large, blond rear end with a bushy black and white tail attached to it. It looked strange beside the long line of elegant, silken beauties.

"It can't be," Bill gasped.

The animal in question lifted his head and looked Bill straight in the eye. His eyes were large and warm, his lips quivered as if smiling, and he nickered "hello" through a mouthful of hay. His black and white mane was clipped short in the standard Fjord Mohawk fashion.

"Whoa, look at him. He's a Fjord." Billy whistled. "Have you driven a Fjord lately?"

"Billy!" Melissa exclaimed.

"What?" Billy asked, his face a mask of innocence.

"Well, I'll be," Bill muttered.

"Did you know that he'd be here?" June asked suspiciously.

"No," Bill and Melissa cried in unison.

"Whoa, boy," June walked forward carefully. Some horses shied away from her canes.

The gelding swiveled his head and dropped his nose down for her to pat. June smiled and moved in closer. He nuzzled her hand.

"Hey, sweetheart. Aren't you out-of-place here?" she whispered in his ear. The gelding snuffled her pant pockets. "Oooh, spoiled too, I see."

"I wonder who the owner is?" Bill looked around. There didn't seem to be anyone looking after these horses. "I'll go see if I can find someone."

"Yessss, that's a good idea," June murmured.

Bill turned quickly and looked over his shoulder. After forty years of marriage, he knew everything there was to know about his wife. That direct, quiet basal tone was all too familiar. The gelding, whoever he belonged to, was coming home with them.

Bill shook his head and chuckled.

"Come on Billy," he tapped his grandson on the head,

"lets go find out who owns this fellow."

Billy grinned up at his grandfather.

"Don't run! Pay attention to your grandfather," Melissa commanded, slapping her son playfully on the behind and sending him on his way. She turned back to her mother-in-law and the Fjord gelding. "He looks just like CD," Melissa commented. "Of course, I never could tell the difference between Chester and CD anyway. They all look alike to me."

"Oh no, they are quite different. This fellow is a much darker brown dun than CD. Look at his stripe, the line on his back, it's almost black. CD's is light brown. The tips of this gelding's ears are almost solid black too; CD's ears are white tipped and then black beneath."

"Okay," Melissa said sheepishly.

June laughed.

"We found him, Gram!" Billy yelled, running down the aisle as fast as his feet would carry him. He slid to a stop, screeching like a racecar, startling several horses on the string. A bay horse with a white half-moon on his face reared and tried to wheel around, but was too close to the other horses to do more than turn his head. He snorted in fear.

"Billy!" his grandfather called angrily. "That's enough!"

"Sorry," Billy whispered, his freckles turning a brilliant shade of red.

"Whoa," a brawny, dark-haired man called out. The horses stopped fretting right away. "Easy does it, Cinder. Steady, Shadow."

He brushed past Billy and gave each of his horses a firm pat. It was clear that he was master to the herd.

"I hear you've an interest in Indy?" the man asked, his

brown eyes glowing with warmth and friendship once he got his string of horses calmed down.

"Is that his name?" Billy piped up.

"Billy! Mind your business right now," Bill commanded.

Billy nodded and bit his lip to keep from blurting something out. Not talking was a hard thing to do.

The man chuckled, and then extended a hand to June and Melissa. They all shook hands.

"My name is Ken Donaldson. These fellows are my string. Indy here has been my packhorse for six years. He's a good boy, doesn't fuss over anything, solid as a rock." The gelding turned and nuzzled his master.

"How come you're selling them?" June asked quietly, one hand still on the Fjord's neck.

"I've been running a hunting and packing outfit for the last ten years, but my wife wants me home more. We have three little ones now. I miss being with them too," he said amiably. "Most of the last four years, I've been taking tourists up into the mountains which is why I switched to the Tennessee Walkers. Lots of them find a gaited horse easier to ride all day than a Quarter Horse. They're all a good, sound lot. Indy packed in all our gear. I could just load him up and leave him loose, he'd just follow along behind. There are pictures of him all over Europe and Japan."

The Stetlers laughed.

"Grandpa, can I ask Mr. Donaldson a question now?" Billy tugged at his grandfather's belt.

Bill raised an eyebrow and nodded. There were smiles all around.

"How come his name is Indy?" Billy asked, his eyes round with interest.

Independence

"Well, his full name is Independence."

"Because he was born on Independence Day," Melissa and June said together.

Ken Donaldson nodded. He looked a little confused. Most people didn't figure it out that fast.

"Whoa. CD is named CD because he was born on Canada Day," Billy said. His mouth fell open and stayed there.

"Close your mouth, Billy, you'll catch flies," his mother said absently.

Billy clamped his jaw shut with an audible click.

"Well, that settles it," Bill looked at his wife. "He's gotta come home with us now, right?"

"You have a horse named CD?" Ken asked, beginning to understand it. "He was born on Canada Day."

As one, the Stetlers nodded.

"And he's another Norwegian Fjord?"

"Yes, he is," June said slowly.

"Well, I'll be," Ken shook his head in disbelief. "My wife's gonna love this story. Kinda fitting, ain't it? When you think about it, you'd have two independents!"

"First things first though. How much do you want for him? I don't expect that there's anyone other than us here who would be interested in Indy?" Bill said, knowing that no matter what the cost, Indy would end up being dropped off by Sam Morrison on his way home.

"Well, just to make things clear. Indy isn't registered and I don't think he can be if that's important to you," Ken said a little sheepishly.

"That doesn't matter to us, does it, Gram?" Billy chirped.

"Billy!" his grandfather scolded him again.

"No, it doesn't," June jumped in. Billy gave her a

26

thumbs-up sign. June grinned.

"Then whatever you are comfortable paying is fine with me. He's a good horse and you seem like fine people," Ken decided. "My wife'll be really happy."

Bill laughed and shook his hand. "Will a thousand do?"

"That's more than fair," Ken agreed. "I'll go and pay his sale fee and withdraw him from the auction."

"What's gonna happen to the others if they don't sell?" Billy asked, his eyes fixed on the blue-black gelding called Shadow, his look as transparent as a lake's surface. Everyone could see that he was imagining himself riding the tall black horse. His mother paled. Even Shadow looked a little fearful.

"If they don't find good homes here, I'll ship them to Kelowna to a friend of mines' spread. Shadow's the only one that's not for sale, young fella. He stays with me. Besides, he's too hot and flashy for a youngster to handle," Ken commented. He smiled at Melissa. She breathed a sigh of relief.

"Do you know if Indy's ever been driven before, Ken?" June asked.

"Yes, ma'am. He was trained to hitch and did real well at it. Fella that I bought him from used to run a carriage service. He did weddings and stuff like that. He had a matching set of Clydesdales and Fjords. He decided to stick to just Clydesdales and sold off the Fjords, that's how I found Indy. He ran a three-horse unicorn hitch with the Fjords. A lady came and bought two, but left Indy behind. I sort'a felt sorry for him, not being chosen first and all. Reckon it's kinda like being the last one picked in the schoolyard. Course it's been five years since he's pulled a wagon 'cause I only did pack trips, but I 'd bet my boots that he'll be thrilled to work as a team again."

"Let's get this deal done, Ken," Bill slapped the younger man on the back, drawing him away from his still nervous daughter-in-law.

Billy darted around his grandmother and lifted a handful of hay to Indy's mouth. Indy snuffled the hay, then rested his nose on top of Billy's head and snorted.

"Oh, gross!" Billy yelled and pulled away, his red hair slick and wet.

"He'll fit in just perfect," Melissa remarked as her cell phone began to ring.

Chapter Three

Susie

The huge black Freightliner with its chrome exhaust pipe running up behind the cab and its shiny chrome grille and side mirrors, rolled into the yard, a long honk from its powerful horn signaling its arrival.

The two sheep let out startled bleats and ran for cover in the copse of fir trees at the end of the pasture. CD hurried to the fence, knowing that the blast meant that Thomas was home. Indy galloped off across the pasture with the sheep, his tail in the air, his mane bristling, honking out a warning that danger was afoot. CD ignored the commotion going on behind him.

"Dad's here!" Billy shouted with glee, letting the screen door slam shut behind him. He jumped off the porch and bolted toward the big rig as it came to a screeching halt, the wolfhound barking excitedly at his side.

The driver's door popped open and a larger version of young Billy stepped down from the cab, his curly carrot colored hair hidden beneath a black Freightliner ball cap, freckles dotting his cheeks, his slate gray eyes reflecting the afternoon sun. He scooped his son up in one easy movement and held him to his chest. Billy wrapped his arms around his father and hugged him as hard as he could.

"You're home," Billy cried happily.

"Whoa, partner, I can't breathe," Thomas gasped.

"Hi, honey," Melissa said as she stepped down from the porch and joined her son and husband in a group hug. The giant dog leaned against Thomas, his tail whipping Melissa's legs hard enough to make her groan.

"Glad you made it safe and sound, boy," Bill said to his son, "any trouble?"

"Why don't you let him come inside before you start talking road trips?" June added, glaring meaningfully at her husband.

Bill shrugged helplessly.

June waited for her turn to give her son a hug and a quick kiss.

The door opened on the far side of the cab and a tall, deeply tanned girl with strawberry blond hair hanging in dozens of tight braids down her back, clad in hip-hugging jeans and a loose cotton shirt, sauntered around the front of the truck. Her lips were pursed in a sour pout and a frown creased her forehead, but even that was unable to hide her beauty. She held a knapsack in one hand and an iPod in the other.

"Susie, come and meet your kid brother and your

stepmother," Thomas waved her forward. "I expect you hardly remember your grandparents, but they do send you some pretty neat gifts every year."

Susie sulked and stood where she was, her feet firmly planted, and her shoulders drooping forward slightly. The stance didn't suit her wiry, muscled frame.

"He's not my kid brother. He's my stepbrother," she corrected her father. "And I have a mother."

"Whatever," Billy replied, insulted. He eyed his half-sister with unease.

"That's enough," Thomas ordered, his face turning red. It was clear that it had been a difficult trip from California and his temper was frayed.

"What is that thing?" she asked, pointing at Horse. Horse's tail stopped wagging and he lowered his head to glare at her through golden-brown eyes. "Is it safe?"

"Horse is an Irish wolfhound and yes, he's safe," Billy said, throwing an arm over the dog's shoulder. Horse licked his face and wagged his tail once, then turned his attention back to the aloof teenager standing before him. "Course that's only if he likes you," he added, under his breath.

"Is that all you have?" June asked, indicating Susie's knapsack, trying to break the stony silence that followed.

Susie remained still, eyes downcast.

"Well, then tomorrow perhaps we girls can go do a little shopping in town," Melissa offered.

Susie stood in silence, neither agreeing nor disagreeing, but keeping a wary eye on the dog.

"She's got a small suitcase in the cab, but I'll bring it in later," Thomas said.

The girl remained mute.

June lifted her gaze and looked questioningly at her

husband. Bill shook his head. They had never had to deal with this before. Thomas had been the perfect son, always working, whether it was for Sam Morrison, his father, or on his schoolwork. He was a popular boy; girls were the only problem, and lots of them.

Other than the gray eyes, strawberry blond hair, and wide face, Susie was nothing like her father. Susie's mother was a lovely girl, but prone to crying. She hated Thomas for leaving her alone with a baby. Eventually, it had cost them their marriage. June wondered if old wounds had festered. Was it that which made her granddaughter so bitter or was it simply a case of teenage rebellion?

CD whinnied and banged a knee against the fence, miffed that he was being ignored. Indy nickered from farther away, standing his ground, watching the scene with interest, undecided on whether to join his new friend at the fence or not, almost as defiant as the teenage girl.

"CD!" Thomas croaked. "I'm sorry, old man, I forgot about you."

Thomas put his son down and jogged over to the fence. The old Fjord dipped his head down and Thomas threw his arms around his neck and gave the horse a big hug. CD snorted. Thomas drew a piece of wrinkly carrot from his back pocket and gave it to the gelding. CD grunted and nibbled on the rubbery carrot, his nostrils quivering.

"How old is that carrot, Dad?" Billy rolled his eyes at his dad. "I don't think CD is impressed."

"Well, it has been in my pocket for two days, but I don't think he minds that much," he winked at his son.

On seeing the carrot being handed to CD, Indy galloped across the pasture and came to a sliding halt beside the older horse. CD pinned back his ears and nipped the younger gelding's neck. Indy backed off a bit, then shouldered his way in to see Thomas, not wanting to be left out, no matter how angry the older horse got. The wolfhound barked once.

"Sorry, fellow, I only brought one," Thomas said, giving the young Fjord a pat.

CD glared at Thomas. Thomas backed up a step.

"Oh, a little jealous, are we?" Thomas laughed.

"Isn't Indy neat, Dad? I just love his haircut. I want to cut CD's mane like that, but grandma won't let me," Billy whined.

June and Melissa laughed.

"I don't think we want you shearing CD just yet," Bill consoled his grandson.

"Susie, come over here and meet the horses," Thomas said to his daughter.

Susie continued to stand where she was.

"What's the matter? You scared of horses too?" Billy asked innocently.

"William Stetler Junior, that's enough," his mother scolded him.

"I'm not scared," Susie said sourly. "I don't like horses. I don't like dogs. I don't like trees. I don't like sheep and I don't want to be here. Does that answer your question?"

"Susie!" Thomas growled.

"Oh my, we do have our work cut out for us," June whispered to Melissa. Melissa groaned.

"So what are you doing here then?" Billy asked, unable to help himself.

Thomas shook his head, not knowing who to spank first, his daughter or his son. Bill put a hand on his son's shoulder and grinned.

"Why don't we all go into the house and have some ice

tea?" June said.

"Good idea," her husband responded. "All this bickering has made me thirsty."

June swatted her husband's arm and started towards the house, her husband by her side. He looked over his shoulder and signaled the others to follow. Thomas pushed up his cap, and then wrapped his wife's arm around his. Billy gave the two horses a final pat, stuck his tongue out at his big sister, and ran after his grandparents. The dog shot Susie a questioning look and then followed the others up to the house, his tail wagging his rump from side to side like a porch swing in a hurricane.

Susie was left standing by herself, watching the Stetlers climb the stairs to the ragged old house with its wobbly porch, blistered paint, and moth-eaten lace curtains. The sun blazed down on her golden locks and mosquitoes swarmed about her head in a whining cloud. She wondered what she had done to deserve this. In California, surf was up, the sky was blue, the wind soft and gentle, and the horizon stretched out for miles. All her friends were at the beach, surfing, playing volleyball, and in general having a great time by the ocean while she was stuck in Hicksville with the musty stink of horse manure in her nostrils and the trees and mountains blocking out the sky. She was sure that the mountains were getting bigger, and closer, and felt as if they were going to squish her like a bug.

Her mother needed to be alone for a while; that's what her stepfather said. Well, if she needed to be alone, then why hadn't he left too? He hadn't been shipped off to Canada. If she was lucky, maybe when she got home, her mother will have shipped her stepfather off some place even farther away, like the moon, or Egypt. Egypt was good, desert, camels and pyramids. In her mind's eyes, she pictured his tall, lanky form stumbling around in the Valley of the Kings, sunburned and lost. Susie chuckled to herself.

Maybe I can hack into the Defense Department's mainframe computer and have him drafted? The thought cheered her. *Markie-Mark could do it! He can do anything with a keyboard. Didn't he manage to change all our grades to B's? The teachers still haven't figured that one out. I think when I get home I'll suggest he change his name to 'Scud II'...search and destroy!*

Susie looked at the house. The dusty windows were vacant. Nobody except the dog seemed to have noticed that she hadn't followed along on everyone's heels like a good little girl. She wasn't little anymore, didn't they get it? She was fifteen. In a year, she could legally move out and live on her own.

"I'll email Mark and ask him for help. Maybe he can score me a plane ticket home," she said to the horse, who eyed her curiously.

Susie swung her knapsack over one shoulder and started shambling towards the house. The two horses whinnied at her, their humongous heads hanging over the fence, their dark eyes observing her. They were the strangest beasts that she had ever seen. The one with the Mohawk was kinda cool, but the other one looked like a Cyclops. It was creepy the way he looked at her with his one good eye as if he could see right into her soul. She shivered. It was even worse than the way the dog looked at her, like she was a pork chop. Hmmm, dinner!

She had been chased on her surfboard by a shark once; that was nothing compared to the way everyone on the farm made her feel.

She shrugged and climbed the stairs to the front porch.

"Everyone has a computer, right?" she said to herself. "I haven't stepped into the Twilight Zone, have I?"

Susie opened the door to the kitchen. Five pairs of eyes, not counting the dog, looked up at her from their seats around the kitchen table.

There was a tall pitcher of iced tea on the table with yellow cornflowers painted on the front. Everyone's glasses were full. There were yellow cornflowers on the glasses too and a plate of homemade peanut butter cookies on a yellow cornflower plate. She was thankful that at least there wasn't a yellow cornflower on the dog's water dish over by the pantry. At least, she assumed that was what the large bucket was. The dog was stretched out under the table. He lifted his head and yawned.

"Oh, my god, I *have* stepped into the Twilight Zone," she muttered and dumped her knapsack on the floor by the door.

Chapter Four

Susie's Big Night Out

Susie lay in her bed staring up at the dark ceiling. Night had fallen. The frogs and crickets in the meadow were competing to see who could croak or chirp the loudest. She tossed and turned, from side to side, and even folded the pillow over her head and held it down over her ears, but no matter which way she faced, or what she did, the noise was deafening.

"Oh, man," she muttered. At least in Venice Beach, she only had to listen to the ocean and the odd siren or gunshot. "Hey, you, Kermit, knock it off. Go find Miss Piggy, or Beaker, anybody, just be quiet!" The frogs kept croaking.

Croakkkk. Croakkkk. Croakkkk.

Susie sat up in bed and kicked away the covers. She

wrapped her arms around her legs and mulled over her choices.

The Stetlers didn't have a computer. She had run out of batteries for her iPod and forgotten her charger so she couldn't listen to her tunes. The nearest store was fifteen miles south. There was nothing to do but sit up in bed and listen to nature in all its glory.

She groaned. *Welcome to the backwaters of BC, Susie girl. My karma must be really bad.*

She pushed back the covers, tugged down her nighty and got out of bed. She walked across to the window and pulled back the lace curtains. A half-moon hung brightly in the sky. In the meadow, misty layers of fog hung suspended in small tufts of cloud above the ground, gathered in hollows, and hovered at the edge of the forest. Susie felt like a fair damsel stuck in a castle waiting for a knight to come and rescue her.

Yeah, like Prince Charming is coming my way. Susie sighed. *Ah, who needs him anyway? I can walk fifteen miles. No biggie. I need batteries. Right now, that's all I really need. Batteries! I'll score some batteries and start hitching home. Who wants to spend a summer with people who name their dog Horse? How sick is that?*

Susie stepped back from the window, grabbed her jeans from the chair beside the ratty wooden dresser that she was sure must be at least two hundred years old, and pulled on a peach colored sweatshirt. A faded picture inside a beat-up oak frame caught her attention. A wispy haired little girl with wide eyes and a great big grin was perched on top of one of the horses. The horse's eyes were dark and kind. The horse looked like he was smiling, like he was posing for the picture, proud to be included in the family photo. A strong, deeply tanned woman with long wavy red hair and a twinkle in her eye held on to the horse. Her cheeks were flushed and she looked not the least bit bent or crippled. She was dressed in a red and black-checkered shirt, faded blue jeans, and black rubber boots. Her grandmother didn't look at all like she did now. Susie wondered briefly which of the horses outside was in the photo? She slipped on a pair of socks, looped her knapsack over her shoulder and, sneakers in hand, snuck down the hallway.

She stopped outside her grandparent's door. Both of them were snoring softly. She could just make out their sleeping forms huddled under the covers in a big four-poster bed. A huge oil painting hung above the bed. The canvas was filled with color, a flower meadow, a stand of white birches, a flat lake with a young doe drinking at its edge. Susie carefully tugged the door shut until she heard the faint click of the latch locking into place. Her stepmother and father were staying in the spare room next door. Their door was shut tight.

She slipped down the stairs in her stocking feet. A couple of the stairs creaked ominously, but no one stirred upstairs. She tiptoed through the living room, around the settee, the china cabinet filled with knickknacks from all over North America including a tiny leather cowboy hat with Texas stitched in red on the brim, a stuffed baby alligator...by far the grossest thing that Susie had ever seen...a pint of maple syrup from Quebec covered in a thin layer of dust, and a cedar carving of a Killer whale.

Her brother was curled up at one end of the couch, his chest rising and falling in a slow and steady rhythm, his legs tucked up to his chin because the dog took up the rest of the couch. The dog rolled his eyes at her as she crept by, watching her with keen interest. The wolfhound let out a long, low yawn.

"Shhh. Good, boy. Stay, Horse," she whispered.

The dog put its head back down on the armrest and wagged its tail once.

"Good, boy."

Susie found her way to the kitchen and let herself out the screen door. She stopped on the porch and put on her sneakers. It was darker than she thought it would be. The mountain looked even closer in the dark; it was a black quilt, a patchwork of dark shadows, its fabric reflecting no light, a mound of rock that was both cold and desolate. Susie shivered.

"Come on, Sus. Batteries. Think 'batteries'."

Susie steeled herself against her fears, cementing her resolve to run...to get away. As her eyes adjusted to the dark, she was able to make out the outlines of the stable roof and the dirt road that led away from the farm. The barn doors were closed, the horses secured inside their stalls, and the sheep asleep inside the shed attached to the barn. June didn't like to leave the animals out at night, especially the sheep.

"So what are you doing out at night if the horses and sheep aren't?" she asked herself. She had no real answer, only that she had to get away from this place.

Susie slung her knapsack over her shoulders and snugged up the straps. The road was a white ribbon under the light of the moon. It reminded her of that old poem, *The Highwayman*. "The moon was a sliver of silver, over the purple moor," she sung. She had always fancied that poem, but never knew why, and struggled to remember who had told it to her. The memory was but a gossamer thread and she let it go, unsolved, undone.

"Oh, well, this isn't that bad," she murmured and

stepped down off the porch.

With a deep breath, Susie started walking down the road towards the highway.

Crickets sung to her as she walked. Frogs croaked, but they didn't seem nearly as loud as when she was trying to sleep. Ground fog curled around her legs like a ghostly cat looking for attention. The bush rustled.

Susie hugged her arms to her chest and increased her pace. Darkness stalked her on either side of the road. The trees were whispering to each other. She wondered if they were talking about her.

You're losing it, kid. Quit that!

She looked over her shoulder and saw the faint image of the white farmhouse disappearing into the distance. She stopped and turned back towards it, took one step, and then shrugged and pulled up the straps on her knapsack. She wheeled around and headed back towards the highway.

A coyote howled in the forest. Another answered.

Susie stopped walking and listened. She was met with silence. Even the frogs and crickets were quiet.

A wolf howled from somewhere up the mountain. A whole pack answered him back. Another lone wolf let out an ear-piercing wail, a desolate wail that sent shivers rippling up her spine. Even the earth seemed to tremble. He was much closer than all the others.

The bushes beside the road shook gently. A faint wisp of white moved amidst the trees. It was a fleeting glimpse, a brief flash, like the image left on the retina after a candle is blown out.

The wind picked up. Tree limbs rattled, leaves rustled. Susie ran for it.

She heard something heavy galloping down the

roadway behind her, heard its raspy breath and the click of claws on gravel.

"Oh, my god, it's the wolf," she gasped, lengthening her stride, running as fast as she could down the dirt road, away from the soft, but urgent, clickety-click-click of the hunter's pursuit. "That's why the horses and sheep are in at night."

Her hair flew out behind her. The knapsack banged painfully against her back. The birch trees that bordered the road looked like white uniformed soldiers, guarding the mountain, their upturned limbs armed and threatening. Chokecherry and Black Hawthorn lined the other side, thorny fingers daring her to try to escape that way.

The wolf was getting closer. Its pursuit grew louder. The scratchy sound of claws on gravel was unmistakable. She heard a growl, felt its hot breath against the nape of her neck. She looked over her shoulder and saw a pair of yellow eyes glowing in the dark, the white flash of fangs, and the silver drip of saliva.

The wolf leapt high into the air, jaws snapping, going for her throat, and then with a startled howl, was knocked to the ground. It tumbled by her in a heap of flying fur and rage. A gigantic, wiry gray form careened past her. It slammed into her hip, toppling her sideways. Sharp gravel tore the flesh from her hands as she skidded down into the ditch.

The wolf got to its feet and stood in the middle of the lane with its head down, drool dripping from its mouth, eyes as bright as Mars, and its snowy white chest heaving, facing the dog, unafraid. Horse snarled and leapt into battle. With one deft movement, he sank his teeth into the old wolf's soft neck tissue and yanked it off its feet. The dog swung the wolf from side to side like a rag doll. The wolfhound outweighed the animal by at least fifty pounds.

Susie screamed in horror.

The wolf yelped with pain. Horse let it go. The wolf sailed through the air, and then landed with a thud on the gravel. It whimpered and staggered to its feet. Horse growled, his teeth flashing, red blood trickling from his jaws. He crouched down low and started to spring forward, ready to finish the hunt, the urge to tear the wolf to pieces bred into him. The wolf let out a soft whimper, its eyes glazed over with pain, its bravery all but gone.

"Horse! No!" Susie yelled.

The dog stopped and glanced her way. Susie scrabbled up the bank on her hands and knees. The wolfhound's eyes were glowing with bloodlust.

"Horse, no! Leave it, please," she begged the dog.

The wolf slunk away into the night, its head and tail down, hungry with defeat. Horse watched him go, the hair on his back standing on end, his muscles trembling, a low growl rumbling from deep inside his throat.

"Good, dog. Good, boy," Susie said, patting her leg, signaling the dog to come.

Horse walked slowly towards her, his head down, his whiskers quivering. He cried when he reached her and laid down, his shoulders and body quaking ever so slightly.

Susie sat on the ground, pain etching a furrow in every fiber of her being, and stroked the giant dog's head. Her hands were raw from road rash. Her right thigh ached painfully from skidding into the ditch. She pushed herself to her feet and carefully put some weight on her right foot. Nothing seemed broken. Her right ankle was throbbing, but it held her weight. She would have to walk back very slowly.

"Well, I guess I really don't need batteries after all."

The dog whined and thumped his tail against the ground.

"I think you just saved my life, Horse." She looked down at the dog. He poked his head under her hand for another pat. Susie laughed. "You deserve a whole lot more than a pat for that, big boy."

Susie bent down and cuddled the dog. She kissed him on top of the head. He licked her face with a raspy tongue.

"Okay. Let's not get carried away. I guess you're not that bad, but I have my limits, understand?"

The dog barked. The frogs and crickets resumed their symphony. Susie turned and limped back to the house, one hand on the dog's back, the wolfhound matching her every step. His eyes roved back and forth, searching the darkness, prepared to finish the job that he had started, ever wary in case the gray wolf or one of its brethren should return.

Susie saw the beam of a flashlight waving around on the porch. Its thin light bounced off the thickening fogbank. The moon was dropping behind the mountain and night was descending as if the last Act was done and the theater's curtain was coming down, signaling the end of the show.

"Horse," Billy whispered hoarsely.

"It's okay, Billy, he's with me," Susie answered, her voice a mere whimper.

"What are you doing out here with Horse?" he asked. "You aren't trying to steal grandma and grandpa's dog, are you?"

Susie snorted and limped towards the light.

"Whoa, what happened to you?" Billy asked, shining the light full in his sister's face.

Susie brushed it aside. Her head hurt enough without having her little brother shining a flashlight in her eyes. She supposed that she must look pretty awful.

"I kinda took a fall."

"Yeah? Took a fall with the dog in the middle of the night? I'm not that dumb, you know?"

"Well, I hope it can be our secret," Susie pleaded.

Billy thought about it for a moment. Horse brushed up against him and licked his face. He giggled. "It'll cost you," her brother said and turned towards the house, one arm wrapped around the dog's thick neck.

"I expect it will," Susie grumbled and followed him into the house.

She tucked her brother back under his blankets, found the box of dog biscuits in the kitchen, and gave Horse a handful. The dog sucked the biscuits up inside his jowls, climbed back up on the couch alongside Billy, and started to chew happily.

"I'll see you in the morning," she whispered to Billy.

"Okay," he whispered back and was fast asleep.

Susie gave the wolfhound another pat and crept upstairs. She snuck into the bathroom and closed the door quietly. When she turned on the light and saw her reflection in the mirror, she was amazed that her little brother hadn't screamed. She had a small cut above her right eye that had left a scarlet trail of blood down one side of her face, her braids were thick with twigs and dead leaves, and both her sweatshirt and jeans were caked with dirt. She started to giggle. She looked like a warthog in a mud hole.

"Well, that's the last time that I decide to walk fifteen miles in the middle of the night to get batteries. I guess I don't need to get home that bad."

The hallway lights popped on.

"Susie, are you okay?" her father asked, knocking gently on the bathroom door.

"Yeah, I'm fine. The frogs are keeping me up," she said through the closed door.

He laughed. "They do take some getting used to."

"I'm just going to take a bath. Maybe that will help. I'm sorry if I woke you." Susie turned on the hot water. She did need a bath, but the dirt wasn't the real reason she needed one. Her body felt like it had been washed, dried, and tumbled. She hadn't hurt this bad since she fell off her surfboard and got caught in an undertow. She had done what she was supposed to, tucked herself into a tight ball, and let the current have its way with her. The undertow rolled her along the seabed for a while, and then relented, popping her to the surface like a cork.

"That's a good idea. Can I get you anything from the kitchen?"

"No, I'm good."

She heard her father go back into his bedroom. From under the thin crack in the door, she saw his light go off. Susie took off her clothes and climbed into the tub.

"There's sure no escaping the Stetler family," she muttered, and slipped into the hot water, the scrapes on her arms screaming anew.

Chapter Five

Company's Coming

June was busy making more pancakes when her granddaughter came down the stairs. The boys had finished the first tall stack as if they hadn't eaten in a week. Melissa kept the coffee cups full and settled into the morning routine, a smile tickling her lips, happy that her husband was home, if only for a short time. Susie slouched into the kitchen and sat down at one of the high-backed kitchen chairs. Her eyes were a bit swollen and she kept her hands on her lap. June thought that a little odd.

"Morning," she muttered sleepily.

"You look like you've been out partying all night," her father said, and then smiled.

"Maybe she was," Billy added cheekily.

Susie fixed her little step-brother with an evil look. He

glared back at her as if daring her to challenge him. Susie's face turned bright red and she glowered at the empty plate in front of her.

Horse stood up under the table and nearly carried the spindle-legged oak heirloom across the kitchen. He looked at June with hopeful eyes and licked his lips.

"I don't think so, Horse. I saw Billy sneakin' you at least three strips of bacon," June said to the dog. He looked at her balefully.

"No, I didn't," Billy whined.

"Billy!" his grandfather scolded the boy.

"What? I only gave him two."

Thomas chortled. "That's my boy."

"Thomas, don't egg him on," Melissa glared at her husband across the table.

"You're in the dog house now, Dad," Billy quipped.

"We don't have a dog house so I don't suppose it'll last for long," his father countered.

"Thomas!" Melissa wagged a finger at her husband.

The men all chuckled.

Horse turned around and wandered over to Susie's side. He lay his head down on her lap and let out a long sigh. Startled, Susie lifted her hands in the air, saw everyone looking at the painful scabs that ran across both her palms, and tucked them quickly under the wolfhound's chin.

"Good Lord, Sus, what happened?" her father asked, standing up.

"I went out on the porch last night and took a bit of a fall," Susie replied, her eyes downcast. Horse snuffled. She lifted a hand out from underneath his head and stroked his wiry coat.

"Yeah, right," Billy sulked.

"Are you alright, honey?" Melissa asked.

"Yes," she said stubbornly, waving her father away as he tried to lift one of her hands for inspection.

June put a new plate of flapjacks on the table. Susie looked up at her, her eyes filling with tears.

"Oh, she's fine, Thomas, stop fussing. Susie's a big girl. If she needs help, she'll ask for it," June nodded at her son. She grabbed up the pitcher of orange juice from the center of the table and filled Susie's glass. Susie smiled at her, a clear look of relief sweeping across her face.

Thomas grunted and sat back down at the table.

"So are you gonna help your mother harness up Independence?" Bill asked his son.

Thomas nodded, but kept a watchful eye on his daughter. The dog looked up and almost grinned at him from his spot beside Susie. Thomas could have sworn that the large wolfhound had just winked at him. He shook his head and turned to face his father while his wife filled his coffee cup.

"We'll hook him up to the manure cart first. That should tell us if he'll take a load. I'd rather have him run away with that, than the wagon."

"I think our Independence will do just fine. He settled in fast and old CD will keep him in line," June said, taking up a seat next to her husband and settling down to have her own breakfast. "I wonder if he was at the front or back of the unicorn hitch."

"What's that, Gram? A uni-thingy-majig," Billy bubbled, a strip of bacon hanging out of one side of his mouth.

"That's a three horse team with two horses behind and one horse in front," his grandmother answered him.

"I expect Indy was in back. He'd have been too young

to be the lead horse," Thomas added.

"That's true. CD will be a good partner for him. I don't think an earthquake could rock that old Fjord of mine, or make him take a misstep."

"Would you like to help?" June asked Susie.

Susie fussed with a pancake, moving it around on her plate like it was an alien life form. Horse nuzzled her hand.

"I guess," she muttered quietly.

"I guess," Billy mimicked her, his father gently slapping him across the back of the head. Horse let out a low woof. Billy grinned crookedly and slouched down in his chair.

The sounds of hoof falls were heard in the driveway. Bill leaned back in his chair and looked through the screen door.

"Well, Billy, looks like you're about to get your first riding lesson. Here comes Andy Morrison and it looks like he's got old Boomer with him."

"Boomer? Can't be," Thomas said, rising from his chair and pushing open the screen door. "Well, I'll be darned, but it is Boomer! I thought that old Appaloosa would be long gone from this world."

Billy bolted from the table.

"Billy!" June and Melissa said together. They looked at each other and laughed.

Billy ran out the door and slid to a stop on the porch. The floorboards squealed.

"Hey, Andy," Bill called a greeting. "Have you had breakfast yet?"

"Well, I've had a coffee," young Andy Morrison said, reining his chestnut gelding up in front of the porch. The red Appaloosa with the white blanket on his hind end stopped obediently.

"Then tie those two horses to the porch and come on in for some flapjacks and another cup of java," Bill advised the young man.

"Wow. Is that really the horse that I'm gonna learn to cowboy on?" Billy piped up, his eyes glowing with happiness.

"Sure is," Andy tipped his hat to young William and stepped out of the saddle. He threw a rein over the porch rail; the chestnut gelding lowered his head and rested one hind foot. The Appaloosa's halter rope was tied to Andy's saddle. The Appy let out a weary sigh and closed his eyes.

"Way, cool!" Billy squawked.

The Appaloosa opened his eyes and glared at the little boy, pinned back his ears and swished his tail. The chestnut lifted his head and eyeballed Billy as if he was glad the kid wasn't his responsibility.

"I see old Boomer has the same bad temperament as ever," Thomas noticed.

"Yep," Andy agreed

"How old is he now, Andy?" Thomas asked, leading the way into the kitchen.

"Twenty-seven."

"And he's still working on the ranch," Bill asked, his voice lifting.

"Only on the rare occasion," Andy answered. He smiled at Billy. "Only when there's young fellas that need some breaking in."

Andy stepped into the kitchen and saw Susie cut a corner off her pancake with a fork and push it around her plate, her soft peach colored braids catching the morning sun like they had been spun with fairy dust. His cheeks burned, the skin flushing to a dark candy-apple red. He quickly took off his hat and hung it on a peg by the door.

Independence

Susie looked up, saw Andy staring, and blushed an even deeper shade of scarlet.

June elbowed Melissa gently in the ribs and nodded towards the two. Melissa smiled and winked at June. Andy Morrison was a fine figure of a young man, just turned eighteen, his curly brown hair cut short for the summer. He walked with an easy gait. A faint smile was fixed permanently to his lips. His face still had the boyish quality of youth, but the handsome man lurking beneath was beginning to show. The effect on Susie was startling.

Susie straightened up in her chair, her eyes alive with interest. She brushed her braids back behind her ears, exposing her high cheekbones, unblemished skin, and the small diamond stud earring in one lobe. The diamond twinkled in the sunlight. She gulped down the last of her orange juice as if her throat was parched.

"You may as well take Billy's seat, Andy. That's the one beside my daughter. I don't reckon that he's gonna leave old Boomer," Thomas pointed to the empty chair at the far end of the table.

"Thank you, sir," Andy nodded and sat down kitty-corner to Susie.

Susie blushed again and looked down at her lap.

Horse ambled over to Andy and laid his head across his thighs, and then lifted his eyes upwards knowingly. Andy chuckled. "Hey, Horse, how's it going? Catch any wolves lately?" Andy scratched the wolfhound behind the ears.

Susie gasped. Everyone looked at her.

"What do you mean 'wolves'?" she stammered, her skin paling and her eyes widening.

"Sorry, miss, didn't mean to scare you," Andy sputtered, apologizing, his face looking equally as stricken.

"I just meant that Horse here is a wolfhound. That's what he's bred to do; chase wolves, I mean."

"Oh, that's all." Susie sighed.

"Were you dreaming of wolves last night, dear?" her father asked, concerned.

"I wouldn't be surprised, not the way they were carrying on last night," Bill added. "I guess that was a first for you, wasn't it?"

Susie nodded.

"There's an old lone wolf out there. Used to be king of the pack, but he's bin forced out now. He took down one of our calves. I'm gonna have to track him down and take care of it," Andy advised the family, his shoulders slumping forward. That was a part of ranching that he really didn't relish.

"Can't have that," Bill agreed. "We'll definitely keep the chickens and livestock in at night."

Susie kept her eyes on the table and her hands folded tightly in her lap.

"Where are our manners?" June asked, changing the subject. "Andy, this is my granddaughter, Susie. Susie's from California. She's come to stay with us for the summer."

"Yes, ma'am, I heard," Andy confessed, his cheeks purpling.

"My but news does travel fast in these parts," Melissa joked, seeing the look in her husband's eye. It was clear he was wondering how many other young men were going to show up at the Stetler's farm. Susie was a very pretty girl. Melissa had a feeling that sending her off with her grandmother to the cabin as soon as Thomas left was a blessing in disguise. Of course, most of the boys around there had horses or dirt bikes. She decided not to mention that fact to her husband and took another sip of coffee.

June pushed the plate of bacon towards Andy. He smiled at her and helped himself to what was left. Susie dug into her pancakes. Thank god for small favors, June thought, the girl was smiling. June went back to the stove and whipped up a few more flapjacks.

"Do wolves often attack people?" Susie stammered.

"No, Miss, they sure don't. They have to be pretty old, real sick, or hurt badly, to bother people. It's unusual for one to be taking down a calf like this, but I've followed this fellow's trail and he walks on three legs sometimes," Andy responded.

"What do you figure caused that?" Bill motioned with a spoon.

"Don't know. Guess the old boy got busted up somewhere. If he can't run down game and has no pack to hunt with, he's gotta look for easy pickings."

"That's really sad," Susie offered.

"Hmm," Andy nodded and lifted a piece of pancake to his mouth.

"When do you plan on driving the cattle up to their summer pasture?" Thomas asked.

Andy stopped chewing for a moment.

"Another week, my dad figures. I'll bring old Boomer down for Billy to ride for a few days and he can ride herd with us, if you like? Boomer'll look after him."

"That's fine with me," Thomas agreed. "Billy will be thrilled."

"Do you want to head up to the cabin then, June?" Bill asked his wife.

"I think that's a great idea. What do you think, Susie? Care to join your first cattle drive?"

"I guess," Susie replied with a shrug, her voice as soft

as a willow's sigh on a hot August day.

"If'n you'd like, Miss, I can bring an extra horse for you?" Andy offered, his eyes fixed on Susie's.

Susie blushed, her cheeks turning a deep crimson.

"I...I don't know," she stammered. "I've never been on a horse...just surfboards."

"I can teach you the same time as I teach your brother, if you want? You can ride King. He's quiet and will do what I tell him to. You'll be okay. It's mostly balance. If'n you can ride a surfboard, then you can ride a horse."

Susie smirked, unsure. Andy was cute, but she really didn't like horses. Of course, until last night, she hadn't liked dogs either and now she had a wolfhound drooling in her lap. Her ankle was still hurting so she wouldn't be walking home anytime soon.

"Fine. Okay. Why not?" Susie hoped she wouldn't live to regret it.

"Let's get a move on and get started," Thomas said, pushing his chair away from the table.

"Is it time?" Billy shouted from the front porch.

"Yep, partner, it's time." Andy chuckled and quickly finished the rest of his flapjacks. "Thanks for the breakfast, ma'am."

"You're welcome, Andy. Anytime you're hungry, you're welcome here," June responded.

Andy followed the men onto the porch, unhitched his gelding's line and unwrapping the Appaloosa's halter rope. The Appaloosa backed up as directed. Andy swung the horse's hip over so that he was standing parallel to the porch.

"Over here, Billy. Put your left foot in the stirrup and swing your leg over. You always mount from the left side of a horse. You too, Miss."

Independence

Billy did as directed and swung up into the saddle with a little help from Andy. He picked up the lead line, a big grin plastered to his face. His gray eyes sparkled.

"Don't I get reins?" he enquired.

"Not today. I'm just gonna lead you around. You can ride old Boomer with a halter as good as a bridle. He's broke to death."

Susie stood on the front porch, her shoulders slightly slumped, the dog leaning against her left hip. She hesitated. A brief look of fear flashed across her face and beaded her upper lip with sweat. Horse never took his golden eyes off of Andy's.

"Don't reckon I've ever seen Horse behave like that. He's sure taken to you fast."

"Thanks. Yeah, I guess so," Susie said, her voice sounding thin even to her. She'd never been afraid of anything before. The horse wasn't that big, just smelly...and hairy...and really dirty. She wondered absently if she should tell Andy about last night, about the wolf...it probably was the one he was looking for. If he found it, would he kill it? Even though the animal had attacked her, Susie didn't want to see it get hurt. You didn't just kill something because it was old, did you?

"Miss," Andy was asking, a confused look in his eye.

What had he been saying to her?

"You don't have to get on King if you don't want to," he said, holding out his hand.

"Sissy," Billy hissed from high up aboard the Appaloosa. Boomer closed his eyes and drifted off to sleep.

Susie straightened up and whacked her brother in the arm as she walked by. The Appaloosa opened his eyes and nuzzled Susie's arm.

"Hey!" Billy sulked, pulling back on the lead rope.

Boomer backed up a few paces.

"Andy's right, Sus. You don't have to learn to ride if don't really want to," her father consoled her.

"No. I can do it," she glanced up at him and her grandfather. Her grandfather grinned encouragement and her father shrugged.

She slipped her left sneaker into the stirrup, grabbed hold of the saddle horn, and then felt Andy's hand on her bottom as he helped her up into the saddle. She arched an eyebrow and glared down at the young man. Andy stuttered an apology. Her father and grandfather choked back a laugh. Pots banged in the kitchen. Susie wasn't dumb. She suspected her grandmother and stepmother were watching through the kitchen window as well.

"So now what?" she quipped.

"Take the reins like so," Andy advised, guiding her hands so that she gripped the reins in her right hand. "And hold onto the saddle horn with the left. You don't need a death grip. It's just for balance to start out."

"What about me," Billy asked, his voice a bit tearful. It was supposed to be his lesson, not his sister's.

"You do the same thing with the halter rope. Hold the rope in your right hand and keep your left hand on the saddle horn." Andy moved over to stand beside Billy. "When you want to go to the right, just slide the rope up his neck on the left side, but make sure you don't pull on his mouth. You too, Susie."

Both Billy and Susie followed Andy's orders. The horses stepped forward in unison and turned to the right.

"Cool," Susie said, her eyes brightening. She tightened her grip on the saddle horn.

"Yee, haaa," Billy hollered, banging his legs against the old Appaloosa's sides. The horse ignored him, but sighed heavily. "Come on, sis, let's race."

"I don't reckon," Andy drawled.

"Yeah. Ditto," Susie added, looking down at Andy. He smiled up at her and blushed again. Susie chuckled. Maybe she was going to enjoy some of her time here.

CD and Independence let out a series of shrill whinnies from their pasture. CD thumped a leg angrily against the fence and licked his lips, his ears pinned back, his nostrils quivering. He glared at the Appaloosa.

"Oooh, that old horse is getting jealous in his old age," June said, leaning heavily against her canes. Standing over the stove for such a long time had made her hips ache. Melissa pushed open the screen door and stood in the doorway beside June drying her hands on her apron.

"CD wouldn't hurt a flea. That's what I love about Fjords, they're so low key, but they certainly have a mind of their own and let you know what's in it," June mused.

"It's okay, CD, I still love you," Billy shouted as he rode by the paddock. "You're the man!"

The old gelding nickered. Independence leaned over the fence and watched the goings on. CD's ears flicked forward and he walked along the fence line, keeping pace with the Appaloosa, Indy following closely on his tail.

CD lifted his head and stared down the road. Indy and the other two horses stopped and looked too. Three more horses with three more cowboys atop of them appeared around the bend in the lane, the soft clip-clop of horse hooves on gravel signaling their arrival. The boys waved a greeting, their eyes widening at the sight of the pretty, athletic girl astride Andy Morrison's favorite gelding. They ribbed each other; Andy never let anyone near King, let alone swing a leg over his back.

CD pinned back his ears and sulked. Independence's

eyes brightened and he arched his head over the fence like a proud lion, the short cropped hairs of his Mohawk bristling. To the younger horse, lots of people and lots of horses meant a trip into the mountains where the grass was greener, the wind was cooler, the water fresher, and everyone made a fuss over him. CD yawned, but kept a watchful eye on the strange horses.

"I can see that I better dig out the coffee urn and set it to perking," June whispered. Her husband chuckled under his breath. Her son's face reddened and his teeth set to grinding.

"Got your shotgun handy, Dad?" Thomas quipped.

"Now, now, son. I recognize that lot. They're good boys. I'd be more concerned with who Susie hangs out with at home in California, than these young men," Bill said to his son. "Wasn't that the real reason her mother sent her up here? 'Beach bums', 'surfer dudes' and 'razzies', wasn't that what she called them? Can't say I know what a 'razzie' is though?"

"I suppose, although, the ones I met didn't seem that bad," Thomas grumbled. "I just remember when Susie was born, so small and fragile. It tore my heart out when her mother moved back to California and took her with her. Susie was only five-years-old. Now I have a beautiful daughter who I barely know, and I have to go back on the road again in less than six days. It just seems like I'll never be a real father to her."

Melissa put an arm around her husband's waist. He kissed her gently on the cheek.

"You're forgetting one thing," Melissa purred in his ear.

"What's that?" Thomas asked, his voice trembling.

"She's her father's daughter no matter what."

Independence

Thomas laughed out loud and switched his attention to the group gathered around his son and daughter. Billy babbled on. The boys laughed and teased the youngster, their eyes fixed on Susie. Susie sat quietly on Andy's gelding, an amused look on her face, Andy close by her side, one hand on his horse's neck.

"I think our granddaughter can take care of herself," June stated.

"I think you're right," Bill said, taking up his wife's hands in his.

"I hope so. At least she seems happy. The trip here from LA isn't one that I'd like to repeat. She tried to run away twice," Thomas confided. "It was like traveling with a rainstorm, complete with thunder and lightning."

"She tried leaving last night too," Bill winked at his son.

"What?"

"Don't worry. We sent Horse after her. He brought her home safe and sound," June consoled her son. "She wasn't gone very long."

"Mom! Dad! She could've been hurt! You heard Andy. There's a rogue wolf out there," Thomas fumed, his eyes narrowing.

"That's why we sent Horse, dear. She needs to want to be here or we're fighting a losing battle and may as well send her back to California with you," June said, squaring her shoulders.

"Yeah, I guess." Thomas let out a heavy sigh, relaxing. "Billy's a lot easier. All you need are earplugs."

June, Bill and Melissa chuckled.

"Yeah, right!" Melissa groaned.

Chapter Six

The Cattle Drive

Andy arrived with the Appaloosa in tow, all saddled up and ready to go. Old Boomer wasn't nearly as quiet as he had been over the course of the last week with young Billy Stetler on board. The big rawboned horse was dancing beside Andy's lighter framed chestnut, the Appy's short cropped cinnamon colored tail slapping his haunches, right to left, then left to right, eyes bright, ears pricked forward. He hadn't been on a cattle drive for several years and he was eager to work.

Susie saw Andy ride in and felt her pulse quicken at the sight of the tall rancher's son moving gracefully in the saddle. For a moment, she wasn't sure if she had made the right decision to accompany her grandmother in the wagon instead of riding out with Andy. She liked Andy and knew that he would be disappointed. Everyone, including her, could see that Andy Morrison was sweet on her, but it was more than a little embarrassing the way her family fawned over him.

Didn't they get it?

She wasn't here for her health or to date some cowboy who smelled of horses, hay, and Irish Spring soap. Susie liked the pungent smell of saltwater, the sounds of seagulls trilling, and the way the gulls hung in the sky over the beach... searching... watching! She loved the excitement she felt when she stared out to sea, searching for the perfect wave, and the skip of her heart when she saw the surf rising. Susie longed to get into her wet suit and feel the gritty, greasy mixture of coconut oil, salt crystals, and sand grains against her skin.

She hated it here in the Interior! Susie wanted to go home and Andy Morrison looking at her with doe eyes wasn't going to change that. *Sooooo...what was she thinking?*

Andy walked the horses up to the farmhouse and dismounted as Billy came running from the house, darting towards him, arms wind-milling.

"Whoa, partner," Andy drawled, tipping his hat to the boy. "You gotta learn to slow down."

Billy grinned and tipped his new hat to Andy.

"So what d'ya think?" Billy asked in a tinny, high-pitched voice.

"That's some hat you got there. Looks pretty fine," Andy nodded.

"Yep. Now I'm a real cowboy. I got me a white hat!" Billy said proudly.

"And you got yourself a fine cow horse too," Andy said, handing over Boomer's reins.

"I sure do. Are ya ready, Boomer?" the boy asked the

gelding. "We got lots of cows to move today."

The Appaloosa snorted and nuzzled Billy's hat. Billy grinned crookedly and pushed him away. The Appy went back to snuffling the small feather attached to the hat's narrow braided band.

"Don't you eat my feather, Boomer, or I'll be mad," Billy chastised the gelding.

Boomer licked his lips and swiveled his head around to watch what was happening over at the barn.

"How about you hold King for me and I'll go help your grandma harness those Fjords?"

"Okay," Billy agreed, thrilled that Andy would ask *him* to look after King. "Don't you worry about King, we're buddies."

Andy flipped Billy's hat down over his eyes and chuckled. Billy laughed and tugged it back up, his eyes gleaming. Having Andy around was like having a big brother, which in Billy's opinion was much better than having a big sister, especially, a big sister who didn't like *anything*.

Andy walked across the yard, heading over to where June and Thomas were just starting to harness up CD and Independence. CD stood quietly, his lead rope tied to the hitching post, while June slipped the wide collar around his neck and attached the wooden hames. The hames looked like a wishbone made of oak. It slipped down the thick collar piece and was buckled together at the top and the bottom with straps. Once done, June slipped on CD's back pad so that it sat just behind his withers and buckled up the bellyband underneath.

"I haven't hitched a team in years," Andy said.

"Not since you were a boy, I bet," Thomas teased.

"Yes, sir," Andy agreed. "That's about right."

Independence

June chuckled as she rechecked the harness for signs of wear before she continued.

"Where's Susie?" Andy asked, trying to appear casual, but not being very successful at it, his flushed cheeks and glassy look giving him away.

"She's up at the house helping her stepmother get the supplies together," Thomas winked. "Why don't you go and give her a hand?"

"Naw. I'll help you harness." Andy looked down at his boots and rolled a pebble beneath one toe.

June and Thomas exchanged a worried glance.

"Billy, bring those horses over here," Thomas waved to his son.

Billy grinned, waved back, and hauled the horses over to the barn. CD and Indy nickered out greetings.

"Can I help too?" the tousle-headed boy asked.

"No, but I want you to watch so that you can help your grandmother when you're up at the cabin," his father replied.

"Okay," he squeaked.

Andy elbowed young Billy gently. The youngster giggled.

"Pay attention, boys." June smiled. She hoped once they got up in the mountains that Susie would start showing as much interest in the horses as Andy and Billy did. June's hands were starting to ache as much as her hips and knees, the arthritis that crippled them moving through the sinews and muscles in her body like a snake slithering through a thicket. Her hands trembled slightly. It was getting harder and harder to paint for extended periods as well.

"Now that we've got the collar and bellyband on, I'm going to roll out the harness strapping. This other long

64

semicircle of leather is the breeching and it rests behind CD's bum, high enough on his hind quarters for support, but not so low as to catch him at the top of the legs."

"What's that for?" Andy asked.

"The breeching helps the horses stop the wagon. See that piece that runs from the breeching strap up over their bums, that's called a hip strap and it holds the breeching in place. Without these straps, the buggy would bump right into the horses' behinds. On our wagon, there is only one center pole so there is a steel cross bar that makes up the double tree at the front of the wagon, one for each horse. Each of those long lines with the chain tugs at the end fastened to either side of the double tree so the horses are balanced when they pull. See that set of rings on the inside of each of the boys' collar? A set of short chains is clipped from those rings to the very front of the center pole. If our wagon didn't have a center pole and was meant for a single horse to pull, there would be a couple of shaft loops on either side of the harness. After Chester died, Sybil Trent lent me her buggy and single harness so I could still get out with CD. Working harness like this one doesn't need those."

"I guess those bum straps are really important then, aren't they? That wouldn't be a good thing, if the wagon bumped into Indy and CD's bums, would it?" Billy asked, his brows knitting together.

"No, that definitely wouldn't," June agreed, swiveling around and fixing her son with a pointed stare as he smothered a laugh. CD turned his head and gently nuzzled June's sleeve. "And it's called a breeching, not a bum strap."

"You okay so far?" Thomas asked the boys.

"Yes, sir," Billy and Andy said together.

"From here, I'm going to fasten on the traces."

"So the horses lean forward and pull with the trace and the collar. The back pad and bellyband help distribute the pull and the breeching keeps the harness in line so that the load of the wagon doesn't bump into their quarters," Andy ventured.

"Yes, that's it," June nodded. "See those rings at the top of the hames and the back pad, the lines, or reins if you prefer, go through there to allow for contact on the bit. With a two horse hitch, the inside rein is hooked to the other horse. CD and Indy must work together to make everything run smoothly."

"Cool," Billy whispered. "You've been doing this a long time, haven't you Grandma?"

Thomas snorted in amusement. CD glared at Billy as if he knew the meaning of his words. Indy looked over CD's shoulder, a sparkle in his eye. Andy flipped Billy's hat back down over his eyes.

"What?" Billy demanded, pushing his hat up with an angry flick, his gray eyes flashing. "What'd I say?"

June laughed.

"Yes, young William, I have been doing this for a very long time."

"That's what I thought," Billy quipped, and then pursed his lips, lost in thought. He didn't know why everyone got so upset by his questions. How was he going to learn anything if everyone got mad at him for asking?

June slipped on CD's bridle.

"How come CD's bridle has those things that cover his eyes? Doesn't that make him mad?" Billy asked, squaring his shoulders, as if daring someone to stop him from asking yet another question.

"Those leather squares are called blinkers. The main

reason for blinkers is so that a horse can't see what's going on behind him, that way he won't get scared and run away with the wagon. They're also to help him focus, so that he's more likely to listen to me when I ask him to do something."

"There's a few ranch horses that could use those." Andy chortled.

"I expect there is," Thomas agreed.

"Not Boomer though," Billy patted the Appaloosa on the neck. "He's not scared of anything."

June walked slowly around CD, one hand resting on his back and shoulder for support, her canes leaning against the fence, and rechecked the harness, starting with the straps, and then the buckles and the hooks. Thomas finished with Indy and rechecked his harness as well.

"Right, away we go. Let's harness these trusty steeds up to their chariot," Thomas kidded.

"Andy, be a dear and fetch CD's old saddle and saddle blanket from the tack room and throw it in the back of the wagon. His bridle is on the horn. There's a small box with brushes and an emergency first aid kit on the floor beside it," June said.

"Are you gonna ride CD, Gram?" Billy asked excitedly.

"No, I'm not going to ride CD." June laughed. "That is so you and your sister can go riding if you want. Andy's father already agreed to leave Boomer's saddle behind for you to use on CD. CD's old western saddle will fit Indy and Susie can ride him if she wants to."

"Like that's gonna happen," Billy sulked, deflated.

"She may change her mind once she gets up in the mountains," June responded quietly.

"How come I can't keep Boomer?" Billy's eyes brimmed with tears.

Independence

"Because you won't need him after today," Andy said cheerily, coming out of the barn with a saddle hitched on one hip. He threw it in the back of the wagon and tossed the saddle blanket over top of it.

"How come?" Billy wondered out loud.

"Because you've done really well riding Boomer, but we need him at the ranch in the summer for small jobs. You can easily handle riding CD. I expect you to ride him quite a lot, even if it's just in the meadow. I'll bring Boomer back for you to ride in the fall when we have to round up the cattle and bring 'em back down."

"Really?" Billy quipped, his tears clearing up.

"Yep," Andy nodded.

Andy took up King's reins and signaled Billy to follow along with him. They moved their horses out of the way as June and Thomas backed CD and Indy up to the wagon. Thomas attached the chain tugs to the double tree while June clipped the front chains to the hooks on the front of the center pole.

"Whoa, boys," June commanded, taking both of CD's and Indy's lines in hand and giving them a gentle tug. Indy tried to step forward, but CD was rooted in place, obeying June's command. The younger gelding quickly settled down.

June let out the lines.

"Whooaaa," she said gently, reassuring Independence as she made her way around the wagon. The horses' ears rotated sideways, listening to their master's voice, and they snorted. CD licked his lips and mouthed the bit. Indy chomped on the metal snaffle in his mouth, nervously chewing on it. June stepped up onto the side step and climbed into the wagon.

"Move your horses farther along, boys, so CD and

Indy can pull out," Thomas advised Andy and Billy before stepping away from the four-wheeled wooden wagon.

June sat down on the padded wagon bench, released the hand brake, a tall lever at the front of the wagon, and picked up the lines. CD and Indy responded to the contact by arching their necks and dipping their heads down, both horses chewing lightly on the bit. "Gid-up, boys," June said, and then clucked to the Fjords.

In unison, both geldings leaned into their collars and pulled the wagon out from under its open-sided shed. Harness jingled and jangled. Horses snorted. The wagon rumbled and squeaked. June smiled as the horses stepped proudly forward, tails swishing, ears up, eager to be traveling.

June drove the wagon up to the house.

"Geeee," June commanded and the horses cross-stepped to the right so that the wagon was even with the porch. "Whoa, boys," she said and the horses stopped, the wagon rolling to a smooth halt. June pulled on the brake and stepped down carefully. She tied the lines to the wagon, knowing that CD wouldn't move a step until commanded. Indy was an amiable horse and took his cues from the much older gelding. He tried to crank his head around to watch June, but CD nipped him, delicately reminding him that he had a job to do.

"Billy, bring my canes with you please," June called to her grandson.

"Okay, Grandma," he yelled and dragged Boomer back to the barn to retrieve his grandmother's walking sticks.

Andy wandered up to the house, King in tow, and tied the gelding's reins to the back of the wagon.

"Billy, keep hold of Boomer when you come back. Stay

Independence

behind the wagon as we load up," Andy yelled.

Billy waved and nodded. With his grandmother's canes under one arm, he tried to get Boomer to trot back to the house, but the Appy was having none of it. The horse plodded across the yard, ignoring the young boy trying to pull him forward. The horse's jauntiness of the morning was gone and he had settled back into his quiet, slightly annoyed view of life.

Susie pushed her way out the screen door, a bundle of blankets and pillows in her arms. She looked at the team of Fjords hooked up to the weather-worn wagon with its flimsy spoke wheels, slightly warped wooden bed, thin high-backed bench seat, and realized she must have some seriously bad karma to deal with. It was either that, or she had fallen into a very bad western movie. Susie grimaced. And her mother worried about sharks and the boys she hung out with?

She saw Andy staring at her and blushed. He blushed an even deeper shade of red, and then looked down at his boots, unable to meet her eyes. She understood then how badly she had hurt his feelings. On looking at the wagon, she wondered if she had made the right choice after all...the ranch horse Andy had offered her looked pretty good right now!

"Just throw everything in the back, Susie," her grandmother said as she walked gingerly around the wagon and climbed up onto the porch.

"The horses aren't going to run away with everything, are they?" she asked, unsure.

"No, dear, the brake is on." June smiled and patted Susie on the shoulder.

"It has brakes?"

"Yes, dear, it does. So do the horses if you know how

to ask," June whispered in her ear.

"Oh."

She looked up. Andy's eyes twinkled with amusement.

"It has brakes," she said to him, lifting one eyebrow, trying to make amends.

"Hmm," he agreed.

Susie smiled. Andy smiled back. He took the load of bedding from her arms and placed it behind the seat.

"Brakes! That's a good thing," she muttered to herself as she went back into the house for more stuff.

Bill, June, Melissa, Thomas, Susie and Andy had the wagon loaded with supplies in no time. Its bed was filled with boxes of food, cans of soup, containers of water, backpacks filled with clothes, and several warm comforters to ward off the chill. The mountains were cooler than the valleys at night, even in July and August. Bill also loaded some dry kindling into the wagon so his wife wouldn't have to worry if the cord of wood that he had left in the woodshed beside the cabin was still a little green.

Susie's face was a layer of confusion. The fact that all the cooking had to be done on a woodstove was just too bizarre for words. She was a smart girl, but the idea that people paid other people for this kind of thing was completely beyond her way of thinking. Canadians were very strange. Who on earth thought cooking on a woodstove and living in a cabin with no electricity or running water was fun? There was no getting around it; Canadians were all completely mad. Susie seriously wanted to get on a plane, a bus, hey, even on a horse, and hitch a ride back to LA.

"Don't forget the bug spray. I don't want to get eaten as bad as I did last year," Billy said. That ought to get his sister going.

"What?" she demanded.

"The bugs are so bad up there that they'll chew you to pieces before you have time to swat 'em," Billy nodded.

"Okay! That's it! I'm not going," Susie said, crossing her arms in front of her.

"Billy!" Thomas wagged a finger at his son.

Andy laughed out loud.

Susie glared at them all.

"It ain't that bad. Your brother's just joshing you," Andy said to her. "The blackflies are done. The mosquitoes only come out at night and there's usually a good strong breeze up there to keep them away. Horseflies can give you a good bite, but they don't bother people much, just the horses."

"You aren't lying to me, are you?" she asked.

"Nope. Cross my heart and hope to die," he said, making the motions.

Susie grunted. She was still not convinced.

"Come on, Susie, climb aboard. I can see the dust on the highroad." June pointed up the mountain.

A wispy cloud of dust rose for a quarter of a mile up the winding mountain road. Even at that distance, they could hear the shouts of the cowboys and the faint moo of the cattle.

"Yeah, my dad's well on his way," Andy responded. "I better get going. I'll see you on the trail." The last part was almost a question and directed at Susie.

"I guess," she answered him back.

Susie stood, feet spread apart, her arms still folded across her chest, looking up at the trail of dust. She fought back tears, not wanting anyone, especially her little brother, to see her cry. She bit her lip. Horse ducked his head under her arms and pulled them apart, forcing her to relax. She chuckled, sniffed, and stroked the dog's wiry head. His tail thumped loudly against a porch beam.

CD snorted and rocked back and forth, ready to be on his way. Indy nickered. Andy untied his horse, swung into the saddle, tipped his hat to everyone and said to Billy, "Up you get, partner, we got cows to move."

"I'm coming," Billy yelled as his father helped him mount Boomer. "Thanks, pa."

Thomas kissed his son on the cheek. "You be good. I'll see you in six weeks when I get back."

"Okay, Dad." Billy wheeled the Appaloosa around and kicked him forward. He jogged along after Andy and King.

"I'll be. My boy's growing up," Thomas muttered to his wife as he watched his son's Stetson dip and weave, in time with the horse's steps, his legs thrust out to the side because of the Appy's wide barrel. It reminded Thomas of one of those funny cartoons that he used to see in the horse magazines he read when he was a kid. Andy rode easily alongside Billy, his legs and hands quiet, spurs softly jingling, lariat rope bouncing against his thigh. Thomas knew that Billy was in good hands.

"Right, son, we'll see you when you get home," June said, turning to hug her son.

"I'll send up a smoke signal...let you know when I'm back," he joked, holding his mother in his arms.

She chuckled, broke away, and kissed her husband on the cheek.

"You take care up there," Bill added quietly.

"Don't I always?" June teased.

He grinned and hugged her again. "I'll miss you. Always do," he whispered in her ear.

"I know."

June let her husband help her up into the wagon. Susie

stared at her grandfather from the far side of the bench seat, her eyes wide like a scared rabbit. June unhooked the reins, released the brake, lifted up the heavy lines, and clucked to the horses. With a grunt of pleasure, they leaned into the harness and pulled the wagon forward. The wagon creaked and groaned. Melissa stood with her arm around her husband's waist watching them go.

Horse yawned, leaned against Bill's leg and looked up.

"Don't look at me like that. You're going with them, aren't you?" Bill asked the dog.

The wolfhound snuffled and licked his hand, saying his own goodbye, and then jumped off the porch, his tail wagging.

"While you're up there, paint me a picture of the lake, young lady," Bill called out to his granddaughter as he waved goodbye. "We still got some wall space left in the kitchen."

Susie swiveled in her seat, but didn't wave back. Her face was ashen.

"They'll be fine, Bill," Melissa said, her voice soft and gentle, the comment as much for her father-in-law's benefit as for her husband's.

June clucked and shook out the lines.

"Trrrottt, boys."

CD and Indy burst into a jog. The sound of rattling chains and wagon wheels bouncing over gravel filled the air. The wagon gently rocked from side to side. The horses snorted and bobbed their heads as the giant wolfhound trotted up beside the older horse, matching the Fjord's gait.

June and Susie traveled in silence.

June let the horses increase their pace, stretching their muscles. She wanted them limber before they turned onto the steep mountain trail. There were several places on the trail that she could halt which allowed them to catch their wind, but it would be at least an hour before the first rest stop.

The sun bounced off the Fjords' shiny coats as their haunches rippled and contracted. Muscles were taut. Black leather harness gleamed, freshly polished. Brass buckles sparkled. The wolfhound's coat looked almost white in the early morning glare.

A fine layer of dust billowed up from behind the wagon and coated the dark green leaves of the shrub alder and hawthorn trees that lined the sides of the road. Wind rustled the branches of the poplar and birches whose canopies shaded the shrubs. The July morning was both cool and pleasant. Too soon, the stifling afternoon heat would shrivel the leaves, bake the underbrush, and coat the horses' chests with sweat.

June sighed with pleasure. She was proud of both her horses. Indy was a perfect match to CD. CD was happy again. His step was high and his eyes were filled with a renewed sense of life. June was glad that they had found Independence. Except for the sullen, obviously terrified girl sitting beside her, life was good.

"Easy, boys. Walk," June called to the Fjords, slowing them into a walk as they approached the clearing where the road branched westwards. "Heads-up, Horse," she warned the dog.

The horses slowed their pace.

The grass in the clearing was trampled flat by a hundred head of cattle. The trail up the mountain branched back in a northeasterly direction. Lodgepole pine and Douglas firs crowded out the birch and poplar farther up the mountain slope, their dark green clusters of needles

Independence

making the mountain appear more menacing than the patchwork quilt of sunlight speckled leaves and sage grasses in the meadow.

"Here we go." June smiled at Susie.

"Okay," Susie whispered back, her long braids bouncing off her back as the wagon lurched sideways. She gripped the back of the bench seat, her knuckles white with tension.

"Haawwww," June commanded, pulling on the left rein and tucking her elbow into her side. The horses stepped to the left and broke into a jog, swinging the wagon outwards. June let them go in a wide arc.

"Geeeee," she called, bringing her left hand back to center and sweeping the right arm back past the elbow. The horses swung to the right, stepping laterally, and swinging the wagon in a tight right-handed circle.

"Way we go, boys. Come on, Horse."

June whistled and clucked, driving the horses upwards. They broke into a trot and started up the mountain trail.

"You want to try?" June asked Susie.

"What? Me?" Susie squeaked.

June handed her the lines, forcing Susie to take them.

"Loop the lines over the top of your index finger, down through the palms, and loop your thumb over top," June told her as a wagon wheel bounced over a rock.

"Like this?" Susie asked, her voice trembling.

"That's it," June answered.

Susie did as directed and held the lines tightly in both hands.

"Ease up and relax," June said as the horses slowed to a powerful, steady jog. "Don't make such a fist."

"Wow, the lines are really heavy," Susie commented.

"That's because you've got a lot of leather in front of you. It's not like having a set of reins in your hands while riding. You need the weight of the lines for balance and pressure on the horses' bits. That's how you control them. If you want to go left, you say 'Haw' and if you want to go right, you say 'Gee'. If you want to slow them down, say 'Easy'. 'Whoa', means stop. Don't open your hands at all. When you pull, pull past your body, not out to the side. We'll just follow the herd slowly. It's going to be really dusty up ahead."

Susie nodded, her shoulders quaking ever so slightly. She took several deep breaths and tried to relax. CD and Indy pulled the wagon up the trail as effortlessly as a truck pulling an empty trailer. Susie marveled at their strength. Neither horse showed signs of slowing. Their breathing was regular and a light layer of sweat darkened their shoulders and chest. The wolfhound trotted happily along beside the wagon, tongue lolling, eyes bright and focused, his tail constantly wagging.

June sat back and closed her eyes, enjoying the warmth of the sun on her face, the smell of the horses, and the gentle wind that ruffled her bangs. The wagon gently rolled from side to side like a fisherman's skiff on a quiet sea. June hummed to herself and let Susie drive, knowing that the Fjords would look after the novice driver.

"This is pretty cool," Susie muttered, after several minutes had gone by.

"Yes, it is." June sighed and glanced sideways. Her granddaughter's lips were curved into a gentle smile and her bronzed cheeks were rosy with pleasure. "Is it as good as riding the waves?"

"Not hardly." Susie let out a deep, throaty laugh. "But it's not bad either."

June laughed as well.

"Let the horses walk on the flatter sections of the trail and jog on the steeper ones. In about an hour, we'll reach a small clearing cut into the side of the trail. You can drive the horses until then. CD knows where we take a break. I don't want to rush too much. The cattle move slowly and the dust is fierce."

Susie nodded, shortened the reins like she'd seen her grandmother do, and yelled, "Gid-up, boys." The horses responded and Susie grinned.

Susie looked to the right and saw that they were already quite far up the mountain. She saw her grandparents' white farmhouse in the valley below and the sliver of gray highway off to the west. The ribbon of asphalt stretched both north and south. The forest stretched up the mountain, northeast and northwest, but to the south, the horizon was a misty haze of heat waves, the valley bottom composed of hay fields, miles and miles of them. Long lines of silver piping attached to huge wheels rumbled across the pastures like spiders crawling across a web. Water spewed out from tall spigots in ever widening arcs.

Susie wiped the sweat from her face with the hem of her T-shirt. The leather lines felt greasy in her hands. The sun beat down on her head and shoulders. She wished that she'd worn a hat, but wouldn't admit it to anyone. There was absolutely no way in the world that she was going to be caught wearing a Stetson.

She could hear CD puffing. His breathing was labored, much fiercer than Indy's. She was about to wake her grandmother, when she saw the pull-over that her grandmother had talked about. It wasn't much, just a widening of the road, but it was well shaded and inviting.

Several tall poplars grew amidst the evergreens, their shivering leaves covering the trail. CD angled towards it, one ear flicking back as if listening for Susie's voice.

"Hawwww, CD," Susie shouted.

The gelding bowed his head, flicked his ear forwards, and stepped farther to the left. The wagon rattled. Horse trotted ahead of the Fjords, and then galloped the final few strides to the first poplar tree. With a thump, he collapsed on the ground, long fingers of drool dripping from his mouth, golden eyes aglow with both happiness and fatigue.

June opened her eyes and straightened up. Her back was sore from slouching in the seat. She hadn't realized she had drifted off to sleep that soundly.

"My, my, my, but my boys are looking after us well," she commented, privately chastising herself for nodding off. Susie wasn't remotely experienced enough to handle trouble.

"Whoa," Susie commanded. The wagon came to a bumpy halt.

June reached over and set the brake.

"Do we need to do anything with the horses?" Susie asked.

"We'll let them have a good breather and towel them off a bit. They can have a small drink of water, but that's it. It's actually only about three hours in total to the lake. There's another rest area in about an hour. It's only because of CD's age that we need to stop. He used to do the whole trail in one go and probably still would if we let him."

"Poor CD," Susie crooned. The old gelding snorted and licked his lips.

June stepped down from the wagon and gave him a

pat, Susie jumping onto the ground behind her. Horse looked up and wagged his tail, but didn't get up. CD swiveled his head around and nuzzled June's arm. Indy nickered softly on the far side. CD's chest was wet with sweat, but not lathered. June slipped a chunk of apple from her pocket and slipped a piece to each of the horses.

Without asking, Susie found an old towel under the seat and began rubbing the sweat from Indy and CD's chests. June smiled and checked the horses' harness. She tightened up one of the traces.

"Are you ready to get going?" June asked her granddaughter, seeing that CD didn't need as much of a break as she thought he would.

"Okay. Can I drive again?" Susie asked sheepishly, shrugging her shoulders.

June burst out laughing. This was a change.

"Hooked, aren't you?"

"Well, I can't drive a car yet, so this will do for now," Susie joked.

"Then when we get back, you can ask your father or your grandfather to teach you how to drive," June added.

"No, they won't," Susie said, her lower lip quivering, knowing that would never happen.

"Look around, dear," June waved at the hundreds of small farms and ranches visible in the distance. "See all those tractors in the fields...the combines...I bet half of those are being driven by boys and girls under the age of sixteen."

"So you really think that Dad would teach me to drive?" Susie shrugged.

"I know he will. Ask him!"

Susie shrugged again, threw the wet towel back under the seat, and climbed into the wagon. "Okay, I will."

June chortled, taking her place on the bench seat beside her granddaughter, and then untying the reins. She released the brake. That was the first time that Susie had called her father, "Dad". Up until now, Susie had refused to call him anything at all.

"Right, here you go then," June said, handing her granddaughter the lines.

Susie lifted the lines and clucked. The horses leaned into the harness and off they went. The dog yawned, stood up, and galloped ahead of the wagon.

At the next stop, they took a longer break and shared a chicken sandwich. Susie marveled at the view and grudgingly admitted that it was very beautiful. The constant wind sweeping across the mountain range kept her cool. She had never skied before, but her grandmother promised that if she wanted to visit one Christmas that they would go to Silver Star Resort for a few days. Surfer Susie on skis!

All too soon, lunch was over and they were off once again.

The sound of mooing got louder and louder. The horses lengthened their stride. A thick dust cloud hovered over the trail. June reached in her pocket and pulled out two handkerchiefs. She fastened one over her mouth, took back the lines, and then handed Susie the other. Susie tied the scarf around her head and tugged it down over her mouth. June handed back the lines, knowing how much it would mean to Susie to be seen driving the horses.

"Oooh," Susie said, wrinkling her nose. She lifted up the lines and slowed the horses down. "What's that horrible smell?"

"Cows," June quipped, her voice muffled by the handkerchief and the loud chorus of bawling cattle. "It takes some getting used to."

"I don't think I'll get used to it. Look! Even CD and Indy are wrinkling up their noses."

June chuckled.

Susie angled the wagon in behind the last of the straggling cows. Mothers and little ones needed a little extra time to walk up the mountain. Stumpy tails swished away black clouds of flies. Calves bawled. The noise was deafening. There were cow pies all over the road, green and noxious mounds. The air smelled like a sewage plant.

Andy and Billy were at the back, barking orders, arms raised in the air, slapping ropes against their legs, driving the cattle forward. Andy looked over his shoulder, saw the wagon, and reined in his horse.

As the wagon pulled up beside him, he nodded at June and Susie, his eyes crinkling over the top of his own bandana. His horse's chest and flanks were covered in a fine layer of white dust, as were his forearms and his shoulders.

"We're almost at the top," he drawled.

"This is awful," Susie said to him.

"Nah, just sticky," he joked. "I'll come jaw with you later, once we've got the cattle settled up above."

"Okay," Susie gave him a thumbs-up.

"See your learning to drive," he nodded towards the Fjords.

"Yeah. It's fun," she admitted.

"I'm gonna remind you of that, real regular like." Andy laughed and wheeled his gelding on its haunches. The dog trotted up beside him. Andy reached down and gave the wolfhound a pat on his way by. King shied and skipped sideways, not sure about a dog that was almost as tall as he was. Several calves saw the dog and bolted forward, terrified of the dust-coated monster that galloped along behind them. Horse ignored the cattle completely, yawned and licked the dirt from his lips.

Susie clucked to CD and Indy. Billy turned and nodded. His face was sour, his eyes red-rimmed and pinched. He had clearly had enough. She almost felt sorry for her little brother; almost, but not much. Susie grinned beneath her scarf. Billy wanted to be a cowboy and now he was. Tough luck! Eat dirt!

She loosened her grip on the lines and let CD and Indy pick their own pace. The sun was unforgiving. The Fjords' chests and haunches were soaked with sweat. Dust turned their pink nostrils gray and blackened their hides.

The forest fell away behind them as the road opened up onto a wide clearing filled with tall, shimmering grasses, and cascades of colorful alpine flowers. Brown and white cattle mooed and fanned out in an ever-widening circle. Cowboys moved off to the side of the trail to let the herd through, their bodies slumping in their saddles. Horses lowered their heads and took a breather. Susie recognized the three boys that had come to visit earlier that week. They tipped their hats to her and smiled a greeting. In the distance, a small lake glittered like a thousand mirrors floated on top of its surface. Set back from the lake was a rustic log cabin, its sides weathered silver, its sagging roof topped with dark gray clumps of moss. It looked sad and lonely, a desolate reminder of the past.

Susie felt her heart sink. Suddenly, she wished the wolf that had attacked her had done its job. Her grandparents' old farmhouse was a palace compared to this.

Chapter Seven

Stetler's Pond

"Ahhh." June inhaled. "Isn't it beautiful?"

"I guess," Susie said quietly, unable to meet her grandmother's gaze. She bit her lip and pushed several layers of braids behind her ears. A cloud of flies buzzed about her head. Swarms of them dotted the rumps of the cattle in the meadow and sipped moisture from the corners of the horses' eyes. CD and Indy shook their heads in disgust.

"Drive the horses up to the front of the cabin, Susie, and we'll dig out some drinks for the boys. I'm sure they could use it."

"Okay. Gid-up, boys. Walk," Susie called, shaking out the lines.

CD and Indy pranced past the cow horses, a little jig in

their step, following the overgrown two-wheeled track that led up to the cabin's front steps. The cow horses barely looked up as the wagon rumbled by. They sighed and closed their eyes, enjoying the brief rest, the only movement the flick of a tail or the blink of an eyelid.

"Come on, boys, we'll get you something to wet your whistles," June waved the cowhands onwards.

"Yes, ma'am," was the resounding answer.

The wagon bumped and thumped its way up to the cabin, the men walking their horses behind it in a weary procession.

"Whoooaaaa," Susie hollered at the Fjords.

The wagon rolled to a halt.

Susie looked over at the cabin and grimaced. A long line of firewood was stacked neatly on one side. The chimney was weathered gray stone and the roof was cedar shake. The cabin was built of hand-hewn logs, each layer insulated by a band of cracked mud caulking. There was a set of willow furniture on the porch: a rocker, two chairs and a rickety table. An old red hurricane lantern sat in the middle of the table, the glass mottled black and the base speckled with rust. A small rectangular outbuilding stood about thirty feet from the cabin, a half-moon carved in its door. On the other side of outbuilding was a pole corral where a wide lean-to squatted in the grass. The lean-to was one-sided and its roof was covered with a thick layer of sod.

"What is that?" Susie asked her grandmother, pointing at the smaller out building.

"That's an outhouse, dear." Her grandmother chuckled.

"You've got to be kidding. I have to go in there?" Susie wrinkled up her nose.

"It's either that or out back with the horses, whichever you prefer," June teased.

"Why is there grass on the roof of that shed?"

"It keeps the horses cool in the middle of the day. In another week or two, it's going to be scorching, even up here. The bush is already very dry. We just haven't had enough snow over the past two winters to keep everything green. Your grandfather and I have been letting the Morrisons bring their cattle up here for the past four years." June lifted the lines from Susie's hands and tied them to the wagon. She slipped on the brake and climbed down to the ground.

"CD and Independence both need very little grass. Those two Fjords will eat themselves to death if we let them so we'll be putting the boys in the corral during the hottest part of the afternoons. They'll go and stand under the lean-to. I'm sure Indy won't stray too far from CD so we'll let them graze in the meadow at night. That way, you and Billy can go riding in the mornings if you want."

Susie rolled her eyes.

Andy reined King up in front of the cabin and stepped down from the saddle. Billy followed the other cowboys over to the corral, his head bobbing up and down with weariness. Horse wagged his tail and wandered off to the corral with Billy. One of the hands helped Billy unsaddle the Appaloosa, and then turned him out in the corral with the rest of the horses to have a roll and a drink of water from the spring that bubbled up on the eastern edge of the paddock.

"Hey, Sus," Andy drawled, wiping an arm across his face. His eyes were red and swollen and he was covered in a white layer of dust from head to foot. "Want some help with the horses?"

Susie looked over at her grandmother.

"Look after your own horse first, Andy. Susie can help me unharness the boys in a few minutes. We'll get some cold drinks out for everyone. CD and Indy will be fine," June nodded towards the two Fjords. CD closed his eyes and rested. Indy swung his head from side to side, not wanting to miss anything.

"Okay," Andy said, shuffling away, his horse ambling along behind him.

"Susie, grab the cooler out of the back of the wagon," June commanded. "I'll back the wagon up beside the porch and then you can help me unhook the team."

"Me?"

"Yes, you!"

"Are you sure?"

"I'm sure." June smiled.

Susie climbed into the back of the wagon and carefully stepped over the packs and boxes of goods that were piled two feet high in the bed. She tripped on a backpack and tilted sideways, her arms wind milling, but managed not to fall. She spotted the blue top of the cooler buried beneath a couple of sleeping bags and dragged it onto the porch. The cooler landed with a heavy thump. Floorboards screeched in protest.

June unhooked the lines and climbed back aboard the wagon, and then backed it in parallel to the porch. With that done, she climbed down and signaled Susie to join her.

"Reach down behind the horses and unfasten the tug chains on the double tree," June directed. Susie glanced up nervously, but June raised an eyebrow and Susie did as she was told.

"Whooaaa, boys," June calmed the horses as Susie

moved from one to the other.

Indy chomped on his bit. CD head-butted the younger horse to keep him in line. June picked up the lines and maintained contact on both CD's and Indy's mouths. She looped the lines over their backs and walked around CD, stopping just beside his shoulder.

"Now, unhook the clips on the front of their collars and ease the center pole slowly to the ground."

Susie fumbled with the clips. CD gently nuzzled her arm as if reassuring the young girl. Indy gave her a not so gentle shove.

"Hey, quit that!" Susie scolded the horse. Indy curled his lip upwards as if laughing at her. "That's not funny!"

"Cheeky, isn't he?" June chortled.

Susie finally got the clips undone and lowered the pole to the ground. June hooked the tug chains to the clip at the top of the breeching strap so they wouldn't catch in the horses' legs.

"Now step aside so I can move them forward. I'll drive them over to the corral and we'll unharness them there. There are hooks to hang the harness on at the back of the outhouse."

Susie moved aside and June drove the Fjords to the corral, resting the lines on CD's back for balance. She called over her shoulder. "Bring me my canes, will you please, Susie?"

Susie lifted her grandmother's canes out from behind the seat and tagged along after the horses, dragging the canes behind her.

"Hey, Susie, nice job," one of the young cowboys greeted her.

"Yeah, you looked good up there. A real natural," another of them said.

Susie blushed, her eyes alight with joy.

Billy glared at her.

Andy smirked, his neck muscles going taut.

Ernie O'Keefe, his father's top hand, elbowed him not so gently in the ribs. Andy grunted and casually wandered over towards the corral.

June slid open the corral's gate and let the Fjords go. Several horses looked up, a couple nickered a greeting, but most went about their business, enjoying the sunshine and the brief rest before they had to make their way back down the mountain.

"Oooohhh, but you were both so good today," June crooned in the horses' ears. They snuffled her hands and licked their lips. June gave them both a good cuddle.

June lifted her gaze from the grazing horses. She saw that the cattle had already wandered deeper into the shady forest. In the distance, the tips of the far-off mountains gleamed like polished silver, their snowy peaks sparkling. Frogs croaked from the cattail-bordered lake and flies buzzed in a sleepy haze around her head. She leaned against CD, already composing her next painting in her mind.

Behind her, she heard voices. She turned and saw Andy and Susie leaning against the fence, watching her.

June gave both her horses a final well-earned pat and limped wordlessly past the young couple, a broad grin widening on her face after she had passed. She rejoined the men.

"So what do you think? Is the ocean as pretty as this?" Andy asked sheepishly. He jutted his chin towards the surrounding meadow and lake.

"It's small. More like a pond really. The ocean is amazing, stretches to forever, always changing," Susie said, lowering her voice. "I suppose it is pretty in its own way though."

She looked at the small cattail bordered lake and the brilliant rainbow of flowers in the meadow, mustard colored buttercups, purple and red paintbrush, and tall clumps of white flowered Bear Grass.

"It's always changing up here too. Every season's different, you'll see. Wait until you see it at night with the full moon on the water, the mist rising in the meadow, the breeze ruffling the cattails," Andy gushed, loving these lands.

"Sorry, it's just not my thing."

"I don't know. Stetler's Pond has a nice ring to it or maybe Susie's Slough."

"Stetler's Pond will do." Susie laughed.

Andy moved a little closer.

Susie backed away.

"I think we better join the others. We have a wagon to unpack."

"I'm not going to hurt you, you know? I'm not trying to...you know...." he said, his feelings hurt.

"You can count on that!" Susie remarked, more coldly than she had intended. She began to walk away, but Andy strode up beside her.

"You're just like a young filly my dad used to own. She never wanted to stop running, but one day, she finally learned that sometimes it's better to stay put than run blindly into one fence after another."

"I'm not running, Andy, and I'm not a horse. This is your world, not mine. I just want to surf and have fun. I want to surf Hawaii. I want to surf Australia. I'm still in high school. Go find someone your own age."

"Maybe I think you're worth waiting for. You aren't

like the girls around here, that's why I like you. I think it's cool you surf and I can even get used to the hair. Well, maybe, not the hair."

"Get a life, Andy," she said, angrily pulling away.

Andy's shoulders slumped in defeat, but then he squared them back up and strode after Susie.

June watched Susie stalk back across the yard, an angry look on her face, Andy walking stiffly behind.

"I'm thinking you're in for a long haul too," Ernie O'Keefe whispered into June's ear.

"I think you're right," she whispered back.

"Come on, Susie, I need some help unloading," June called to her granddaughter.

"Yeah, why don't *you* do a little *work* for a change," Billy sulked, throwing a rock at the porch.

"That's enough, young man," June glared at her grandson.

Billy twisted his face into an ugly grimace. The wolfhound got up and leaned against him, almost knocking him over.

"Horse. I'm too tired for that," Billy whined.

"Go and grab some ice tea and sodas for everyone, Billy," his grandmother suggested.

"Why can't Susie go get them?"

"Because I have to help Gram," Susie said, swatting him on the behind.

The cowboys chuckled and rolled their eyes at each other. This was more entertaining than an afternoon watching soap operas on TV.

"Come on, Billy. I'll help you fetch the drinks," Ernie offered. "You did a man's job today, boy. You should be proud."

"Really?" Billy beamed.

Independence

"Yep," Ernie nodded and placed a hand across the young boy's shoulder, drawing him away from the crowd of cowboys sitting on the ground in a semi-circle, chewing on blades of grass, or leaning back against their saddles and relaxing.

Within the hour, Andy and his cowboys were mounted on their horses and ready to ride back down the mountain. Billy ran into the cabin, unable to watch Andy ride away with Boomer in tow. Susie lounged in a chair on the porch, earplugs firmly tucked in her ears, iPod cranked up so that she didn't have to talk to Andy.

"I'll be up to check on the cattle in a few days. I'm sure my mom will send a care package," Andy said to June, his gaze focused on Susie.

"I'm sure she will. Thanks for all your help, Andy."

Andy looked forlornly at Susie, and then spun his horse on its haunches and galloped off after the others. Ernie tipped his hat to June and rode after his boss.

"That was rude," June scolded her granddaughter.

"I can't hear you," Susie shrugged.

June tugged the earphones out of Susie's ears.

"Now you can!"

"Owwww."

"That was extremely rude."

"I know," Susie said guiltily, "but better to break his heart now than later."

"Is that what you call it?"

Susie put her earphones back in.

June gazed sadly down at her granddaughter until the sound of breaking glass made her scurry into the cabin to check on what kind of damage Billy had just done.

Night settled in.

June and her grandchildren sat at a log table, playing cards by candle light. June's canes were propped against the old steel framed bed in the corner. Open cupboards were lined with boxes of food. The dog slept on the floor amidst the sleeping bags.

"I think the two of you should go fishing tomorrow. It would be nice to have some fresh trout for dinner."

"Great," Susie said. "Where's the spear?"

"A spear? What for? The trout aren't that big," Billy said, his eyes growing big.

"That's how I fish, don't you?" Susie replied in earnest.

"How do you get the worm on the end of it?"

June started laughing. Susie and Billy started to laugh too.

"After we've speared all the trout in the pond, maybe we can go riding?" Susie suggested.

Billy abruptly stopped laughing.

"I don't have a horse," he said, softly.

"Ride double on Indy. I'd say ride CD, Billy, but the trip up the mountain took a bit too much of a toll on him."

"Sure wish I had Boomer."

June re-dealt the cards. They played in silence for awhile.

"Fish!" Billy yelled.

"You cheated," Susie joked.

"Did not."

June chuckled.

"I bet Andy will be back tomorrow or the next day," Billy jeered.

"That's nice," Susie countered, not rising to the bait.

"Susie and Andy up in a tree," he sung.

"Billy!" June scolded.

Independence

"Don't even go there, squirt," Susie growled, playfully ruffling his hair.

"Susie and Andy up in a tree," he sang again, this time much more softly.

Susie dove for her little brother. Billy howled with laughter and ducked away. Chairs tumbled to the floor. The dog leapt to his feet, growling.

"Okay, okay, enough already, you two. You're both monsters," June commanded.

Susie continued to chase her brother around the cabin, over the bed, around the dog. She picked up a pillow and slammed it against his head. Billy slammed her back. The dog barked and nipped at their heels.

"Stop!" June yelled.

Susie and Billy stopped fighting, their breathing coming in hard, short puffs.

June dodged around them, grabbed a pillow off the bed, and swung it at her grandson.

The fight was on.

Feathers flew everywhere.

Around midnight, June felt a small tug on her nightgown. She opened her eyes and saw the small beam from a flashlight illuminating Susie's panicked face. Behind her, the dog's eyes glowed yellow in the dark. He watched them intently. Billy slept through the intrusion.

"What's the problem, dear?" she mumbled sleepily.

"I have to go pee," Susie whined.

"Just take Horse with you when you go."

"But…," Susie stammered.

"But what," June asked, trying to hide her annoyance.

"What if the wolf is out there?"

"Horse will protect you."

"What if there are cows between here and there? What if there's a bull with them?"

"This from a girl who fishes with a spear gun?"

"I know," she pleaded.

"Sorry, kiddo. You have a flashlight. You have Horse. Unless you want to hold your water until morning, you're on your own."

"You're a mean grandma."

"I'm a tired grandma," June mumbled and rolled over.

Susie crept to the door. She thought of waking Billy, but then thought better of it. He'd never let her live it down.

Horse yawned and stood up.

"Come on, boy, it's you and me and the great outdoors, at night, in the mountains," she squeaked.

The dog wagged his tail and led the way out the door.

Susie exited the cabin, the thin flashlight beam trailing over the dry ground as the wolfhound jogged into the night. There was no moon. An endless carpet of stars blanketed the sky.

"Horse, come back here," she whispered hoarsely.

On command, the dog appeared out of the pitch black, his eyes looking eerily frightening in the reflection of the flashlight, his grey coat disappearing into the darkness that stretched out behind him.

Susie could smell the horses and taste the dew on her lips.

Every sound was amplified. Frogs croaked. Crickets chirped. Night birds twittered. A cow mooed somewhere across the pond.

Susie took a tentative step off the porch and stopped short. All she could think of was the rogue wolf and how lucky she had been that first night at her grandparent's farm when she thought she could walk out to the highway, and was almost killed.

She instantly lost her nerve.

She hiked down her pajamas and peed into the dirt by the front step, keeping a watchful eye on the dog. Once done, she darted back to the house as fast as she could, the dog hot on her heels.

Chapter Eight

Better than Birthdays

Life settled into a quiet rhythm over the next few days. June was glad of the break in the fighting between sister and step-brother. Every so often, they even seemed to really enjoy each other's company.

The sun was a big round ball of fire in the sky. It scorched the earth below. The air was hazy with heat.

Susie and Billy saddled up Indy.

"I'm steering," Billy said.

"Oh, no, you're not."

"Fine, but I am not sitting on the saddle horn again," Billy argued. "I still got bruises from yesterday."

"Then you'll sit behind me, where you belong."

"Fat chance of that," Billy wailed.

June sat on a stool in the shade of the cabin, an easel in

front of her, listening to the pair quibble. She sketched a picture of the kids and Independence.

They finally mounted: Susie in the saddle and Billy behind her, his legs sticking out sideways, his arms wrapped around Susie's waist, holding on for dear life. They waved at June before trotting out of the yard and off across the meadow, the wolfhound galloping along happily beside them.

CD whinnied and galloped across the paddock.

June put down her pencils and walked over to her old horse.

"CD," she cooed softly.

The horse trotted over to her. She rubbed his nose and kissed him gently on the nose.

"I know, sweetie, but our days of galloping across the meadows are done, old man."

The horse nibbled on a strand of June's hair. She laughed.

"How about I give you a good brushing? How's that sound?"

The horse snorted. June leaned her canes against the corral fence and reached for the box of curry combs that the kids left beside the fence. She ducked under the pole corral and began to give the old horse a good rub down. She hummed softly to herself as she worked.

The old gelding nickered.

June looked up, startled.

In the distance, she saw Andy astride his big Quarter horse, King. The Appaloosa trotted along behind him. A large bag hung from the saddle horn. He loped over to June.

"Howdy, Mrs. Stetler. Mom sent up some fresh ribs and steaks for you. She thought you might like some fresh food. There's some tomatoes and fruit in here too."

"You give your mother a big hug for me."

"I will."

"I see you brought Boomer back."

"Dad says we can live without him, but Billy can't."

June burst out laughing. "Billy's going to be mighty happy to see that old Appy."

Andy looked around, searching for Susie.

"They just rode off. You can probably catch up to them."

"Naw, s' alright," Andy drawled.

"Don't give up on her, Andy."

Andy sat quietly in the saddle. June put down the brushes and climbed under the poles. Andy handed her down the bag of food.

"Go throw CD's saddle onto Boomer's back and go find them. I expect, in this heat, the cows won't be far from the south end of the lake. You'll probably find them there."

Andy thought about it for a moment, and then slipped down from the saddle. He tacked the Appaloosa up, tipped his hat to June, and swung back up onto King's back in one easy movement, before galloping across the meadow, the Appy racing behind.

"Was I ever that young, CD? Wait! Don't answer that." June chuckled as she watched the young man disappear around the far side of the lake. "You know I made Bill work real hard at it. Did I ever tell you that I almost married Andy's father's older brother instead of Bill?"

The gelding snorted in answer. June grinned and picked up her canes, before hobbling off towards the cabin with her bag of fresh groceries.

Independence

Independence picked his way slowly along the mountain trail. Cattle grazed peacefully along the slopes. The wolfhound startled a few of them, but the dog was more intent on sniffing the trail than chasing after cows.

"See that cow over there?" Billy pointed towards the mountain.

"There are lots of cows over there."

"The one with the nose ring and bald face?"

"What about her?"

"That's not a 'her', that's a 'him'. That's Frankie, short for Frankenstein. He's a bull and he's mean."

"Wise words, Yoda. I shall stay far away from Frankie."

"Funny, but I don't see Bella. She's the second in command. Where she and Bossie go, the others follow," Billy said knowingly.

"That's cool."

"Andy told me that every herd has a lead cow and all the others look to her for telling them what to do. He says that they're lucky because they have two."

"They've got the last word, huh?"

"Yep, they sure do," Billy squirmed.

Andy trotted around the bend. Independence spun towards him. Billy squealed with delight.

"Andy! You brought Boomer."

Andy grinned as he trotted up beside them. The wolfhound barked a greeting.

"Susie," Andy tipped his hat to her.

"Andy," she remarked casually.

"We can't find Bella, but everyone else appears to be here," Billy prattled on.

"She should be calving soon," Andy responded.

"We've been keeping a good eye on the cows for you,"

Billy crowed.

"Glad to hear it."

"Why don't you slip off Indy and mount Boomer? We'll go look for Bella."

"Okay, Andy," Billy said, eagerly slipping off the Fjord and taking Boomer's reins from Andy.

Billy crawled up a boulder and jumped aboard the Appaloosa.

The three rode up the trail together. The cattle ignored them, content to just fill their bellies on the plentiful grass.

"You guys haven't run into that wolf at all, have you?" Andy asked of Susie.

"I saw some tracks down by the lake this morning, but didn't see nothing," Billy quipped.

"Those weren't wolf tracks, those were Horse's, Billy," Susie corrected him. "And it's 'didn't see anything', not 'didn't see nothing.'"

"Uh, unh," he insisted.

"So you're an expert now?"

Billy sulked.

"I don't know about the English part, but I expect Billy knows the difference between wolf and wolfhound tracks, Susie. I don't mean to call you out on it, but Billy's lived here all his life. If he says there were wolf tracks by the lake, then I believe him."

"Horse'll fix him if he comes around, won't you Horse?" Billy said to the dog.

The dog whined and wagged his tail in agreement.

Susie rode on, strangely quiet.

Andy wasn't sure if that was a good thing or a bad thing.

They continued to ride up a long gulley that looped back towards the lake, until they came upon a cow lying on the ground, a large brass bell around its neck. The cow bellowed in pain; its coat slick with sweat.

"Bella!" Andy exclaimed, swinging his leg over top of the saddle and dismounting. He dropped the reins to the ground. His horse stood quietly, ground tied, waiting for his return.

"What's the matter?" Susie asked, breaking her silence.

"I think we have a breached birth."

"What's that?"

"The calf is twisted the wrong way in the uterus," Andy advised the two of them. Andy knelt down beside the cow, cooing to it softly. He gently rolled his hands over the length of Bella's stomach. "Yeah, the calf is breached."

The dog nosed after the cow, who bellowed even louder.

"Out of here, Horse," Andy commanded.

Susie dismounted. She handed Billy her reins. The dog lay down on the ground, close to Billy and the horses.

"Can I help?" Susie crouched down beside Andy.

"Hold her head for me. Just talk to her quietly. I've got to try and turn the calf."

Billy held on to Indy and Boomer's reins, and with the other hand he stroked the wolfhound's head, both frightened and fascinated by what he was seeing.

Susie knelt down beside the cow's head. She reached out to calm the cow and got head butted in the process. She tried again, crooning softly to the cow until she was finally able to get a hand on its neck.

Andy stood up and walked over to his horse, leaving Susie softly whispering nothings in the cow's ear. He grabbed his canteen and washed his hands off as best he could, and then slowly made his way around the back of the cow. He knelt down and reached inside the cow, gently feeling around until he found the calf.

"That is so gross!" Susie turned her head away.

"That ought to do it," Andy said, gently straightening the calf so that it would come out the right way. "Has to be done."

"I think it's cool," Billy piped up, his voice rising in the excitement.

Andy stood up, his arms coated in blood and liquid.

"You can leave her be. Nature'll take its course now."

Susie let go of the cow's head and stood up.

Andy walked back to his horse and rinsed his hands off with the last of the water in his canteen. He then pulled a towel out of his saddle bags and wiped his arms.

The three of them then stood together and watched as Bella gave birth to a beautiful red and white calf.

"That really is incredible," Susie confessed.

"And yucky," Billy chimed when he saw the afterbirth sac splatter on the ground.

"Good job guys. Let's leave momma be now," Andy said, mounting King.

Susie climbed aboard Independence and Billy walked along until he found another large boulder, and was able to jump onto Boomer.

The three rode away in silence, Susie turning in the saddle every so often to watch the calf caper around on its spindly legs.

Andy, Billy and Susie rode into the yard, the dog running ahead of the horses. CD whinnied a greeting as he trotted over to meet them.

June emerged from the cabin.

"Andy, you want to stay for dinner since it was you who supplied it?"

"Love to, thank you, ma'am."

"Grandma, we saw a calf being born," Billy stammered.

"It was really cool," admitted Susie reluctantly.

"Andy had to reach inside the cow and everything. It was way gross."

The three dismounted and start un-tacking the horses.

"Well you better make sure you wash up real good, young man," June said to Andy.

"Yes-um." Andy grinned.

Around the table, hands were steepled in prayer. A rack of grilled ribs and a big bowl of mashed potatoes steamed heavenly goodness. Freshly sliced tomatoes and cucumber were laid out on a plate beside them.

"Thank you, Lord, for all this bounty, for the good neighbors who provided this bounty, and for nice young men like Andy who deliver that bounty to our table," June said with some mirth.

"Don't forget King," Billy chirped.

"And thank you, Lord, for Andy's horse, King, who brought Andy and the bounty up the mountain and delivered that bounty to our table."

They all shared a laugh.

"Amen," they said as one.

Susie and Andy exchanged a look. Andy smiled as soon as he caught Susie's eye. Susie looked down at her empty plate and smiled too.

June smiled, noticing the exchange, and then started to dish out potatoes, but wisely said nothing.

Billy missed it all as he quietly counted the ribs.

"Pass around the tomatoes, Billy."

"Yes, Gram."

As dinner was dished out, June found her peace. She had all that she dreamed of and more. Her family was pulling itself back together. She prayed that their good fortune would continue.

The moon rose over the lake. Moonlight sparkled on the water. Bull rushes swayed gently in the summer breeze like hands upturned to the beautiful goddess in worship, celebrating the glow that she cast upon the night.

Warm, soft lantern light poured from the cabin windows. A shadow appeared out of the darkness, stalking towards the cabin. The wolf's fur glowed ghostly silver as it passed the horses in the corral, not a sound marking its path.

The horses sensed its presence and spooked. They galloped to the far end of the corral, trumpeting a warning. King slid to a stop, reared, and struck out with his front hooves, snorting aggressively.

The white wolf stopped at the lake and stooped its head to drink, ever watchful for the only predator it truly feared: man. It glanced towards the cabin, its yellow eyes glittering like opals. It startled but did not run as the cabin door flew open, and light cascaded outwards.

Andy stepped outside, rifle in hand.

"You think it's him?" June asked from inside the cabin.

"Not sure."

"Be careful," Susie said nervously. "There's no 911 up here."

"I will be."

"Can I come to?" Billy chirruped hopefully.

"No," Andy, June, and Susie barked in unison.

Andy stepped off the porch, walking a little farther into the night. The wolfhound appeared by his side and growled menacingly. Andy grabbed hold of the dog's collar.

"He's out there, isn't he, boy?"

The massive wolfhound rumbled in answer and bared its teeth.

"Well, now's not the time, not unless it goes for the horses."

Down the by the lake, the wolf, sensing the wolfhound's presence slunk away, disappearing into the long grass that bordered the lake. It was not ready for a fight that night as its leg had still not yet healed from where the wolfhound had sunk its sharp teeth into its hind quarters and neck.

The horses instantly settled down.

The wolfhound lay down beside Andy's feet, its eyes ever watchful.

Andy too sensed that the threat had gone and relaxed. He gave the dog a pat before turning back to the cabin.

"I know the moon is bright, but I think maybe you should roll your bedroll up beside Billy's and stay the night, Andy. It's too dangerous for you to ride off home by yourself tonight," June said worriedly.

"Yes, ma'am, I won't argue with that," Andy responded. "I did let the evening get on more than I planned."

"You would have ridden back down the mountain in the dark?" Susie asked, amazed.

"It's a good road and the moon's high in the sky at this time of year. I'd have been fine. It's quite beautiful. You should join me sometime."

"You know why you don't surf at night?"

"Why?" Billy and Andy asked together.

"Because sharks swim in to shore at night to feed."

The wolfhound rumbled as if in agreement with Susie.

"But there's no such thing as land sharks, are there?" Billy asked fearfully.

"No, there's no such thing as land sharks," June assured her grandson.

Billy was visibly relieved.

"I'll just go grab my bedroll then." Andy grinned.

"Not without Horse," Susie demanded.

"So you do care?" Andy murmured.

"I'm just not sticking my arm up places where the sun don't shine or going riding down a mountain in the middle of the night with a man-eating wolf out for blood," Susie said definitely.

"Come on, Horse, we got to go walk someplace where the sun don't shine." Andy laughed as he headed for the door. "And we have to check on the horses while we're at it."

"Keep your Winchester close," June advised.

"Yes, ma'am."

"You know this is better than a birthday," Billy said happily.

"How's that?" June asked puzzled.

"I saw a calf being born. Boomer's back. A wolf didn't eat him. There's no such thing as a Land shark. Andy's sweet on my sister. My sister's trying not to like it," Billy teased, skipping out of reach of both June and Susie as they both tried to swat him. "Definitely, better than a birthday."

Chapter Nine

On the Hunt

Andy sat atop King, Susie standing to one side, rubbing the horse's nose.

June watched the two of them from out the cabin's window. She had kept Billy inside to help with the dishes, wanting to give the two of them a moment of peace. It was clear to June that Andy didn't really want to leave.

"Are you going to hunt that wolf?"

"Have to. You and Billy stay off the trails today and for the next few days. I don't want to have to worry about you. I need to check on the calves. We can't afford to lose them to that darned wolf and he'd kill them for sure."

"Andy," Susie muttered softly, her voice trembling. She knitted her brows together, readying herself for his anger.

"Susie?"

"I've seen him. It was Horse that hurt him." She bit her lip.

"What do you mean? When did this happen?"

"The first night I was here. I snuck out. I needed batteries."

"You needed batteries," Andy said, tipping his hat back on his head. He was flabbergasted.

"I didn't want to be here. I wanted to go home."

"And you needed batteries to do it?"

"No, the batteries were for my IPod."

"Oh, you had me worried there," Andy joked sourly.

"A white wolf attacked me. Thank god for Horse. Horse beat him up pretty bad."

"I'm glad you told me," Andy answered huskily.

"You aren't mad at me, are you?"

"You aren't gonna do it again, are you?"

"Lord, no."

"That's good. This isn't California. There are more dangerous things than rogue wolves out there," Andy said, wagging a finger at her.

"No worse than gang bangers," she replied, grabbed his finger and pinching it.

"Be safe," Andy cautioned, pulling his finger back before she ripped it right off his hand. He chuckled.

"Ditto."

Andy paused before pulling King backwards a step.

Susie looked up, wondering if he was going to try to kiss her again, but he didn't.

"I won't see you for a week or two. I've got hay to bring in and it's all hands on deck."

"Okay," Susie squeaked, hating herself for the sound of disappointment that had crept into her voice. *Seriously, what had gotten into her?*

"Okay."

Andy backed up his horse, wheeled around, and then loped off.

June walked out onto the porch.

"I'm glad you and Andy seemed to have worked things out."

"I wouldn't go that far," Susie responded huskily.

June laughed merrily. Susie couldn't help but join in.

"What did I miss," Billy asked, scooting onto the porch like it was a skating rink.

"Nothing," Susie quipped.

"You joshing me?"

"Why would I josh you?"

"Because you're real evil sometimes," Billy said, eyeing his sister critically.

"That's because I'm a Land shark," Susie said. She put her hands in front of her face and opened and closed them like jaws. She snapped her teeth together.

Billy squealed with delight and then ran past her into the yard. Susie ran after him, all the while opening and closing her imaginary jaws.

June chuckled.

"Oh, this is going to be a long day," June muttered, and walked back into the cabin, leaving the pair to amuse themselves outside.

Andy galloped around the back of lake, the lake that he now thought of as Stetler's Pond thanks to Susie. He smiled. She really was different from all the girls he had met.

He went through all the words that described her in his mind: proud, fierce, brave, beautiful, stubborn, athletic, beautiful, fearless, and beautiful.

He laughed at himself as he rode on. He was doomed and he knew it.

He reined his horse up at the spot where the long grasses along the water's edge had been trampled into the mud. He saw the distinct impression of wolf tracks in the dark earth. There were other smaller tracks left by coyotes and raccoons as well, but the white wolf's track was larger than all of them.

Andy followed the wolf's tracks up to a game trail that looped back into the canyon to the north where he had caught up to Susie and Billy on their ride the day before. The thought of Susie having to protect herself and her little brother set him on edge. Horse would give his life to protect the two of them, he knew, but even the giant wolfhound alone might not be enough to stop this wolf in particular.

This wolf was rogue. It didn't behave like other wolves. It preferred solitude over running with a pack. That made it dangerous. It seemed to fear nothing.

Andy pulled his rifle from its sleeve. He rode with one hand on the reins. The other hand was wrapped tightly around the rifle stock; the rifle perched upwards, resting on one leg, ready to fire.

Andy circled through the woods and over top of the low slopes, studying the cattle in the grassland below. He was annoyed. He had lost the wolf's tracks in the hills. He stopped on a rise.

Below him, the cattle grazed peacefully, but he didn't see Bella and her new calf anywhere.

He rode back down into the low valley and circled back across his tracks and into the dead end canyon where

Independence

Bella had given birth.

He heard the bawling of a calf ahead of him and the trumpet of warning from its mother. He raced towards the sound, putting his spurs to the Quarter horse.

Andy galloped around the bend.

The white wolf, its chest dotted with dried blood stains and its hindquarters stained equally dark, went for the calf, teeth gnashing. Bella stormed the wolf, trying valiantly to protect her baby.

Andy fired off a warning shot.

The wolf stopped its attack in mid-air.

The cow head butted it and rolled it across the ground.

Andy's horse slid to a stop. He lifted the rifle took aim and fired. The bullet ricocheted wide off a rock near the wolf's head.

The wolf stumbled to its feet and ran up the rocks, heading for the high ground.

Andy took aim again and fired.

The wolf veered to the right.

Once again, the bullet went wide.

Andy galloped to the cow and dismounted.

"Whoa, Bella, easy girl," he crooned to the heavily breathing cow. He checked her throat and neck to make sure the wolf hadn't bitten her. He was relieved to find the cow none the worse for the encounter.

He then checked on the calf.

The calf bolted around him and ran to its mother's side.

Andy could see that it too was unharmed.

"You two need to get back to the main herd," Andy chastised the cow. "It's not like you not to stay with them."

Andy rubbed the cow's head, and then returned to his horse.

He mounted up and slid the rifle into its leather scabbard. He then pulled out his rope and slapped it against his knee.

"Come on, girl, off we go. Haw," he shouted.

Bella mooed and moved off down the canyon.

Andy continued to drive her until he reached the main herd. He sat in the saddle for a moment, watching over his cattle. He took a swig from his canteen and looked to the hills. The wolf was long gone, but he was still uneasy about leaving the herd. He thought of staying one more night, but there was too much work to be done at the ranch.

Andy dismounted and ground tied King. He opened up the container that housed the egg salad sandwich that June had made for him. As he ate his sandwich in silence, his mind drifted to thoughts of Susie. He smiled and rested, gazing out at the mountain pastures.

Above him a hawk circled. It swooped out of the sky and landed amidst the un-grazed pasture, flying off with a mouse in its talons.

Good for the hawk, he thought, bad for the mouse. Mother Nature was a cruel mistress.

Andy laid his head back on the ground, pulling his hat down over his eyes. He was comforted by the thought of Susie worrying about him riding alone at night and found his heart soaring as high as the hawk, but he also knew the moon would light his way and his rifle would be at the ready.

The sun dipped down below the horizon setting the sky on fire. Andy jogged through the hills mounted aboard the sure-footed gelding, making one last patrol around the herd. All was quiet. There was no sign of the wolf. The herd was relaxed and so was the big Quarter horse beneath him.

As he headed home, he made a wide pass of the cabin.

Boomer whinnied when he caught the scent of his herd mate, King.

Andy saw a candle flickering in the window and wished with all his heart that he could stop and spend another night in Susie's company. If he didn't return tonight though, his father would send a posse out to find him.

He rode on, his heart thundering in his chest. To him, it sounded even louder than the chip-clunk of King's horseshoes on the dusty trail.

The three quarter moon rose high into the sky, lighting up the trail that flowed like a dusty river down the mountain. Towering trees lined its banks on either side. Tendrils of fog snaked around his horse's hooves.

King snorted and jogged lightly down the mountain, his neck arched, nostrils flared. Andy rode easily in the saddle, his rifle perched across one knee, ready to fire if needed.

For the first time in his life, Andy found the ride lonely, and wished the dreadlocked girl with the smoldering eyes was at his side.

Chapter Ten

Summer's Inferno

Unable to stay cooped up any longer, Billy and Susie rode out together a few days later, Billy on Boomer and Susie astride Independence. June didn't know who enjoyed it more, her bickering grandchildren or her happy-go-lucky Fjord and the old Appaloosa.

Susie was still terrified of using the outhouse at night and tossed and turned inside her bedroll on the floor, steadfastly refusing to believe that she wasn't being attacked by hordes of spiders as she slept. Billy delighted in tormenting his sister by putting beetles, spiders, and even a slimy garter snake, under her sheets every chance he got.

On the days that Andy came to visit, Billy still tended to sulk. As far as Billy was concerned, he had met Andy

Independence

first, and Andy should be paying attention to him, not Susie. The rivalry for Andy's affections prompted numerous arguments and even more bugs in his sister's linen.

Andy's regular visits were causing a remarkable change in Susie. At first, the changes were subtle. Susie took out her braids and let her hair fall over her shoulders in a silken wave. The annoying silences that Susie fell into sometimes stopped completely. She put her iPod into her backpack and left it there. She stopped complaining about the smell of the wood smoke from the stove and even offered to help clean the dishes.

One bright sunny afternoon, Susie surprised June by picking up a paintbrush and painting a small picture of the pond on the back of a piece of birch bark. The picture was quite good. Susie said she was going to give it to her mother when she got home.

That was by far the strangest event yet. Susie's mother had not called once prior to their heading up the mountain, nor had she yet to call Thomas or Bill according to Andy's news from home. Susie had phoned home four times before they left, but always got an answering machine, or so Susie said. When June asked Thomas about it, he didn't seem surprised. Thomas shrugged and got a dark look on his face that said he didn't want to talk about it. After the last unanswered phone call, Susie had run crying to her room. The tears, of course, had been followed by two days of stony silence. June stopped suggesting that Susie call her mother after that.

Her granddaughter proved to be a resilient girl though, and on the whole, the summer was turning into one of the most pleasant ones that June had ever spent at the cabin.

June was just putting the finishing touches on her painting, and then dipping her brushes in the glass jar of turpentine beside her easel, when a wave of thunder shook the valley.

The sky turned an ominous black. Thickening clouds and jagged streaks of blue lightning flickered between the clouds like bolts of molten fire. An early darkness settled over the late afternoon, smothering the daylight. The horses huddled under the lean-to, the wind in their faces, their eyes alert, and their ears pricked forward. The sage grass in the meadow rippled and sighed, the wind bending its brown and withered stalks against its will. The flowers in the meadow had gone to seed, except at the outer boundaries of the newly christened, Stetler's Pond. The summer had turned into a real scorcher. June didn't remember ever seeing the water so low in the lake.

She had started to really pay attention to the dryness all around them several days earlier when the deer came down out of the forest in droves, lowering their heads gracefully to sip from the muddy edges of the now shrinking lake. They came to slate their thirst at all hours of the day and night. Even the sight of the giant wolfhound sleeping on the porch didn't seem to bother them. The coyotes came too...and their larger counterparts...but the wolves tended to visit only at night, their wide paw prints unmistakable in the soft muddy shore of the lake.

June stood under the porch eaves and shaded her eyes with her hand, her paints and easel now tucked safely in one corner of the cabin. The wind whipped whirlpools of dust around the yard. At least fifty head of cattle had gathered at the far side of the meadow, keeping to the trees, their brown and white hides visible beneath the thin limbs of the white birches.

Independence

June knitted her brows together. She had wandered up to the edge of the forest that morning, Horse at her side, and noticed the crackle of dead grass and needles beneath her hiking boots. If lightning struck, the forest would ignite, and so would the withered grasses in the meadow.

Susie ambled out onto the porch and slipped an arm under her grandmother's.

"Wow. What a show!" Susie exclaimed, her eyes reflecting yet another round of lightning.

Thunder rumbled. The earth shook.

"It is. I think we're going to have to pack up and head home early," June said, patting Susie's hand. "The forest is too dry to handle any lightning strikes."

Billy came out and stood with them, his cheeks smeared with chocolate from a giant double chocolate chip cookie.

"Awww," he said through a mouthful of cookie, "I'm having fun."

June stifled a chuckle. Her grandson was chocolate from cheek to cheek, nose to chin.

Thunder crashed.

The horses whinnied. The dog whined and leaned against Susie's leg, his head hung low, his eyes glazed, and his tail tucked between his legs. Susie stroked his head absently.

"What about Andy's cows? We can't leave them?" Billy chirruped.

"They can look after themselves," his grandmother said, absently.

Susie looked down at her little brother. He met her steady gaze, a knowing look passing between them. They would do whatever they had to in order to protect Andy's cattle.

"Don't even think about it," June said, glaring at her grandchildren.

Susie and Billy blushed a deep shade of purple. It was eerie how their grandmother always seemed to know what they were thinking.

"We'll start packing up the smaller items tonight. Yes, my mind's made up, we're going home tomorrow," June declared, her eyes narrowing. There was no room for argument.

Lightning crackled, jagged bolts leapt from cloud to cloud. The wind picked up and lashed the pond into a roiling cauldron of leaves, brown water and green scum. Out in the pasture, the horses squealed in fright and galloped through the open gate of the corral and into the lean-to shed.

"What about the horses, Gram?" Billy yelled over the howling wind.

"They'll be fine. The lean-to will keep the worst away from them," June nodded, and then bit her lip. At least, she hoped it would. She knitted her hands together and quietly prayed for the storm to blow over quickly. The horses stood inside the shelter, heads up, looking towards the cabin, almost as if they too were looking to her for reassurance.

Lightning crackled all night long. June, Billy, and Susie sat at the small wooden table playing cards, the sound of the howling wind and the giant claps of thunder making it impossible to sleep. The wolfhound shivered and slunk around the cabin with his tail between his legs. Susie wanted to go out to check on the horses, but June wouldn't allow it. Strike after strike of jagged lightning struck the ground; they stopped counting at twelve.

Independence

By daybreak, the storm had dissipated, but thin rivulets of smoke were already drifting in from the surrounding hills. The sun was a muted lantern, a dull and lifeless orb within a rice paper shell. The smell of charred trees clogged the nostrils and stung the eyes. The forest fires were moving closer. The cattle in the meadow were gone, their tracks embedded in the mud, traveling south, heading down the mountain. The herd was taking itself home. June gave the evacuation order!

Billy opened the door and darted past June, running for the corral.

"Billy! Stop!" his grandmother called after him.

The young boy ran to the paddock. The lean-to was empty. Two sections of fence poles lay broken on the ground, and the surrounding area was a muddy quagmire.

"Grandma, they're gone! CD, Indy, and Boomer have all run away," Billy screeched, his eyes brimming with tears.

"How're we going to get home?" Susie asked, her lips trembling. Her eyes were black rimmed and glassy with fatigue.

June limped off the porch, her hips aching, her back bent. She walked over to the corral, saw the broken fence, and looked toward the mountaintop. A layer of smoke hung like ground fog in the meadow, but she could still make out the tips of the surrounding mountains. She pursed her lips and let out a piercing whistle.

A sharp whinny echoed across the valley.

June whistled again.

CD came barreling out of the stand of birch and alder on the far side of the lake. He screamed a greeting and galloped across the meadow, his hoof beats as loud as the thunder had been during the height of the storm. The gelding slid to a stop in front of June and nuzzled her arm, his nostrils flared.

"Good boy, CD. Where's Indy and Boomer? Aren't they with you, old man?" June crooned to the gelding. He snuffled and cuddled up to her.

"Grandma, we have to try and find Indy and Boomer," Billy whined. "What'll Andy say if I don't bring Boomer home?"

"Yeah, and CD can't pull the wagon by himself," Susie said, her voice quaking.

"No, he can't," June agreed. She rubbed the old Fjord's neck and gave him a quick kiss.

"Billy, go fetch a halter," she ordered her grandson. "Susie, you grab the other two. I want you to go see if you can find the horses. Start walking in the direction that CD came from, but if the smoke gets too thick, I want you to come back immediately. Don't be out more than an hour. If you can't find them by then, we'll start heading down without the wagon. I'm sure that the Morrisons will already be heading up this way to check on their cattle and to check on us too. Indy and Boomer have probably already headed back home."

"Okay, Gram," Susie said.

Susie followed Billy to the corral and snatched two of the halters off the fence. Billy ran back to CD with the other rope halter and slipped it over the old gelding's head. Horse stood to one side, his eyes fixed on the growing clouds of smoke drifting into the meadow. He whined and looked up at June.

"Why can't I go with Susie?" Billy asked tearfully.

"I need you to help me with CD," his grandmother said. "You'll have to hold him for me while I get things packed and keep talking to him, keep him calm. I'll load

Independence

up what I can into the wagon in case Susie does find Indy. If not, we're going to have to saddle CD up real quick and leave without it."

"Oh," Billy said, his lips quivering.

"It's okay, Billy, I'll find them," Susie consoled her brother. "I promise."

"Cross your heart and hope to die?" Billy sniffled.

"Yeah," Susie said, making the motions.

Billy nodded.

"You be careful. Remember if the smoke gets thicker or you hear crackling or you feel a rush of hot wind in your face, you run back here as fast as you can. Understand?" June said. "Horse, go with Susie, bring her back safe!"

Susie spun on her heels and took off at a run. The dog barked and sprinted across the meadow after her. Susie looked up into the hills; the smoke was thick over the forest, wispy gray tendrils wandered down the mountain in gossamer threads.

"Devil's hair! That's what it is," she murmured to the dog. Deep golden eyes observed her. The dog snorted in agreement. "We're gonna lose everything, Horse, if we don't at least find Indy! All of grandma's paintings! Our clothes! Everything!"

Susie's shoulders shook with grief.

"I bet it was Andy's favorite old cow, Bossy, that led the herd back to the lake. Bella hasn't been doing her job since she had that calf. If I can find Boomer, maybe we can push the rest of the herd down into the bottom pasture. What do you think, Horse? Think we can do it?"

The dog barked and wagged his tail. She wondered what her friends in LA would think of her now. Who would have thought that she would care about a bunch of cows?

A horse whinnied off to her left. Susie stopped and listened.

"Indy! Boomer," she shouted.

A giant hulk bulldozed its way through the patch of alders in front of her. Behind the bulldozer trotted a sour-faced, pink-eyed Appaloosa. The Fjord jogged over to her and head butted the tall teenager, the relief in his eyes clearly evident. He sighed with pleasure and dipped his head into her arms for a welcoming pat. The wolfhound jumped out of the way as Boomer swung his hips around and tried to boot him. A night in the bush had made the old horse grumpier than ever.

"You guys had us worried silly." Susie patted them both, and then slipped a halter over each of their heads. Indy snorted with pleasure.

Susie started to lead them back towards the cabin when she heard the terrified bawling of cattle in the distance. Boomer skipped sideways, his eyes rolling in his sockets, the whites exposed. The dog whined and hung his head.

"No way can we leave them," Susie said, straightening her shoulders. "This is probably the dumbest thing that I've ever done, but Boomer move your bum over by that rock, we're gonna go save those cows. Indy, you'll just have to stick with us."

Susie untied the lead rope on Indy' halter and wrapped the loose rope around her waist several times. She pushed Boomer's hind end over so that he stood parallel to a large boulder, climbed onto the rock, and then swung a leg over the Appy's back. Susie grabbed a handful of mane and steadied herself as the gelding danced on the spot, his shoulders trembling.

"If I can ride a surfboard through a pipeline, I can ride

you bareback," she muttered to the Appaloosa.

She dragged the lead rope up his neck, intending to use it as a makeshift rein, and then squeezed her legs together. The Appaloosa moved forward and turned right as commanded. She flipped the lean rope over his head and tried turning him left just to make sure the horse was listening. The well broke cow horse responded to the slightest of pressure. Susie teetered to one side, righted herself, and took a deep breath. The Appaloosa settled down.

"Okay, guys. Let's do it!" she said, squeezing her legs together and taking up a handful of mane.

Boomer trotted forward, across the lower pasture, and up the steep mountain trail that opened up before them. Indy trotted after the Appaloosa, leaving the large wolfhound to bring up the rear.

The geldings' hooves dug into the parched earth, the grasses dead and lifeless. The hillside around them was barren of all except the hardiest of weeds. The horses bolted up the hill, pink nostrils flaring, sweat glistening on their chests and flanks. They were both big, rangy horses, built for rugged terrain. Metal horseshoes clanged, steel striking stone, as they moved upwards on the rocky mountain trail.

Susie reined the gelding in. She stared into the forest. The smoke at the top of the hill was as thick as London fog. *Maybe this was a real dumb thing to do.*

She heard the sound of choppers buzzing overhead and the low hum of water bombers as firefighting teams descended upon the mountain. She prayed that the firefighters had already picked up her grandmother and little brother. If they had, then it was up to her to get the horses to safety. She had grown too attached to the two

Fjords to let them burn to death on top of this mountain and there was no way that she was going to leave Boomer behind.

Susie kicked the gelding forward.

"Come on, cows, where are you? I don't have much time," she said, looking around.

Susie's chest burned; her lungs rattled. The thickening smoke was making it harder and harder to breathe. The horses weren't fairing much better. Their eyes were weeping and the trot up the trail in the simmering heat was taking its toll. Susie knew they were strong horses and would give her everything she asked for, but just how much more could they take? Boomer was tiring. He was starting to stumble.

The frantic sound of mooing was getting closer and she sank her heels into Boomer's sides. Amidst the noise, Susie heard the distinct chime of Bella's cowbell. He leapt forward at a gallop, Indy and the dog hot on his heels.

"Whoa, Boomer," Susie called, lifting the lead rope and sitting backwards. The Appy planted his hind legs and skidded to a halt, Independence nearly plowing into his behind.

"Bella! God bless you, you smart old thing, you wouldn't leave this lot alone," she said to the cow standing on the far side of the brackish water hole. The herd of Herefords was scattered amidst the trees behind Bella and her calf, milling in circles, their eyes filled with terror.

"Let's move 'em out, boys," Susie said. "Sic those cows, Horse." The dog looked at her as if she'd lost her mind. He was a wolfhound, not a German shepherd or a Border collie. Susie laughed and reined the gelding in behind the brown and white cow.

"Hee-up, Bella," Susie hollered, lifting one arm in the

air.

Bella let out a long, low rumble of protest and ambled forward.

"Hup, Bella! Gee-up!" Susie screamed. "Come on, Horse, think Border collie! You can do it. If not, just stare them down!"

The dog growled and ran into the bush. The nearest cow saw him and bolted around Independence. The young Fjord stood in the middle of the trail with a confused look on his face as if he wasn't sure which way to go or who to follow. With a snort, he let out a buck and trotted up beside Boomer.

The lead cow started to move, her giant, fat body rolling from side to side as she walked. She bawled out another call and the rest of the herd tucked themselves in behind her. The cattle flicked their tails and nervously licked their lips, the big wolfhound tracking their every move.

Susie noticed that one young heifer was staying back from the herd. She trotted over to the cow and saw a newborn calf lying on the ground. Innocent eyes looked up at her.

Susie slipped off the Appaloosa, making sure to keep hold of the lead line. The back of her jeans was stained brown in a horseshoe shaped ring, small red hairs sticking out of her jeans like tiny porcupine quills. She picked up the calf and cradled it against her chest. Its coat was still wet and sticky from being born. She pushed aside the heifer's inquisitive nose. The calf nuzzled her and tried to suck on her chin.

"Stop that you," Susie scolded the calf. He let out a sad little 'bleep'.

Susie chuckled and led Boomer over to a rotted stump.

She hoped that she could get back on him without losing the calf. She stood on the stump and draped the calf over the gelding's shoulder, and then swung herself up onto his back. The gelding swiveled his head around and shot her a disgusted look. With the calf safely cradled in her arms, she squeezed her legs together and they were off. The heifer followed along behind them, not wanting to take her eyes off her baby.

Snap! Crackle! Hiss!

The fir trees to the southwest erupted into flames. Boomer screamed and reared. Susie grabbed hold of his mane and held on tight, trying to balance herself and the shifting weight of the calf. The calf slipped sideways. She tugged on the calf's hind end and righted herself.

"Whoa, Boomer!" she yelled.

The gelding snorted, his eyes rolling in terror, his breathing ragged, but he stood his ground bravely. The dog started barking crazily.

With a loud 'swooshhhh", the forest in front of Susie erupted into a fiery ball of flame. The cattle bawled in terror. Independence snorted and reared. The gelding screamed. A ring of fire surrounded them, red hot and deadly! The brackish water in the pond reflected the lights from a thousand yellow candles. Susie held her breath. They were trapped!

"Oh, God. What have I done? There's no way out!"

Susie whirled the Appaloosa in a tight circle. The air was blistering hot, but her skin felt like ice as shivers rippled through her slender body. The firestorm roared like Niagara Falls. Trees exploded. A fetid wind seared her face. Susie felt like her lungs were caught between two vises.

"Lord, help us. Boomer, we're not going to make it!"

Independence

Susie cried, dirty tears streaking down her face, her hands shaking uncontrollably as she held the calf tight to her breast.

A chopper buzzed overhead. The call signs stenciled on its tail read AEC 298. Its yellow and blue striped sides were dirty and stained; black exhaust billowed from its single engine. The side door slid open, a yellow hard hat poked out. A soot-smudged face looked down at her. The chopper hovered in the air several meters above the tree line, a bucket hanging on a line underneath it, swinging back and forth, water dripping from the trap door in the bottom. The firefighter leaned out the door and waved at Susie.

Susie lifted a hand and pointed down the trail.

"I need to go that way!" she screamed over the roar of the fire and the 'thwap, thwap," of the chopper's blades.

Boomer danced on the spot as Independence ran circles around him. The dog hunkered to one side, trying to avoid the flying hooves of both horses.

The firefighter nodded. He turned his head and said something to the pilot. Susie watched, valiantly keeping hold of Boomer and the calf. Her arms felt like lead. She wanted more than anything else to be rid of the calf's dead weight.

The horses shook with fear, their chests and shoulders frothy with white foam. The cattle ahead of them were shrieking in terror and milling this way and that, not knowing which way to run.

The chopper circled around. It dropped its load of water on the trail in front of her. The fire hissed and spat like a threatened cat! The chopper swung lower and hovered there. Susie nodded and waved at the firefighter.

"I ain't stupid, we're out of here," she shouted, and

then grinned stupidly. The firefighter grinned back and gave her a thumbs-up! Susie briefly returned the gesture.

"Hey, cows! Hah!" she yelled until her voice was hoarse.

Susie used Boomer as a battering ram and slammed him into the old cow's buttocks. Bella grunted and leapt forward. Susie laced the cow on the hindquarters with the end of the lead rope, all the while holding onto the bawling calf. Bella ran blindly up the trail, the herd stampeding after her.

Susie heard the low drone of a large plane and looked up. A water tanker crested over the tops of the burning forest. The giant, square coffin-like plane was a sight for sore eyes. It opened its doors and a cascade of fire retardant fell from the sky in a red wave. The flames ahead of her were beaten down.

"Yessss!" she screamed and galloped onwards.

A second plane flew in and laid another trail of red through the bush. Susie ran on, the Appaloosa surging forward, his haunches rippling, Indy galloping behind him, the Fjord's breath hot on Susie's neck. She lost sight of the dog, but knew that he would be close at hand. A couple of steers, their eyes wide with panic, knocked the Appaloosa aside and bolted ahead of them.

The trees lining the edges of the line of red retardant burst into flames. Susie, the horses, and the cattle, ran on, heedless of the burning bushes to either side of them. The two steers in front of her skidded to a halt as a great wall of flame rose high into the air, blocking their escape route.

The chopper swung in and dropped a load of water on the flames. The cattle milled about in a circle, too scared to run through the opening. Susie was caught in the middle of the frightened herd, unable to whip the cattle forward.

Independence

The pilot saw what was happening and dipped the chopper's nose. He revved the rotors, carefully trying to push the frantic cattle forward without causing them to stampede over top of Susie and the horses.

Bella bellowed and bolted through the opening, the rest of the herd following her. The chopper backed off.

Susie galloped headlong into the meadow, the calf still balanced over her thighs, her knuckles white, her fingers knotted in the Appaloosa's mane, her legs wrapped around his belly, holding on for all she was worth. Indy burst out of the brush behind them and galloped up beside the Appaloosa, matching his pace, his head held proudly in the air, his tail streaming out behind him. Horse ran full tilt after the two horses, his tongue lolling, drool flying from his lips, his long legs matching the horses' wild pace. Cows, steers, and calves ran as fast as their legs could carry them; their stomachs stained red from the fire retardant.

Susie slowed Boomer to a canter. She looked down and saw that his four white socks were also a brilliant shade of red, as were her running shoes and the lower half of her blue jeans. The calf on her lap bounced and bawled for its mother.

Boomer snorted and gave a little buck, happy to be free of the inferno. The Appaloosa's chest heaved; steam rose off his flanks. Susie reined him in, allowing the old cow horse to catch his breath.

Indy bolted on by them, heading straight for CD. CD whinnied a greeting and pranced on the spot, lifting up his head and swinging Billy in an arc. Billy's runners left the ground, the young boy not wanting to let go of the lead line.

Susie trotted over to her grandmother. Her grandmother's mouth fell open in astonishment. Susie swung a leg over the tired horse and slipped to the ground, the calf still in her arms. She lowered the calf and let it go. Its mother galloped towards them, flicking her tail, glad to have her baby back. The calf wobbled to its feet and immediately started to suckle. Susie kept a tight hold of Boomer's lead rope, her legs shaking with fatigue. The Appaloosa lowered his head in exhaustion.

"Good Lord, Susie. What were you thinking?" her grandmother muttered, pulling the young girl towards her. Tears glistened on her cheeks. "I thought I'd lost you."

The chopper buzzed overhead, and then turned to hover in the air, close enough that Susie could see the firefighter and the white-helmeted pilot, but a safe enough distance away not to spook the horses any further. The firefighter and the pilot waved to her. Susie waved back, and then gave them a thumbs-up. They returned the salute and then returned to the fire that was still burning uncontrollably in the hills.

Susie realized that she owed her life to those men! She hoped that one day she would be able to say, "Thank you!"

"Come on, I know you and the horses are exhausted, but we have to get out of here," June cried. "Let's get CD and Indy harnessed."

Susie nodded and gave the Appy a much-deserved pat on the shoulder. It was then that she saw the speckled patches of burned hair on his hindquarters.

"Oh, Boomer, I'm so sorry," she cried tearfully.

The Appaloosa raised his head and brushed his nose against her arm. His shoulders were wet with sweat, the skin quivering. Susie laid a trembling hand on his neck and stroked him gently. He smelled of perspiration and burnt flesh.

"Susie, we have to go! He'll be okay. We'll tie him to

the back of the wagon," her grandmother consoled her.

Susie sniffed and nodded her head. June wrapped a protective arm around her shoulder and guided her granddaughter and the Appaloosa over to the wagon.

A 205 helicopter circled and landed in the meadow on the northern most side of the pond, eight firefighters streaming out of its belly. The men and women were dressed in bright orange coveralls and lemon yellow hard hats. They hauled pumps and hose out of the chopper and started to work setting up a fire line.

"Billy!" June shouted over the din of the forest fire and the whine of the chopper. "Get a line on Independence and hold onto him while I harness him up."

Billy's eyes were as wide and wild as the cattle dodging out from under the chopper's circling blades. He shivered and shook. CD nuzzled his arm, gently bringing the boy back to reality.

Susie removed the lead line from her slim waist, clipped it onto Indy's halter and pushed it into Billy's hands. He stood there, looking up at his big sister, his eyes brimming with tears, CD appearing to guard his back. Indy nuzzled the older horse and stood quietly beside Billy, his chest heaving.

"It's alright, Billy. I'll help harness, you just hold the horses."

Billy shrugged and tried to smile at his big sister. She patted him on the shoulder and ran for the two sets of harness.

"I'll take the collars and hames, you grab the harness," June wheezed. "We'll get the bridles last."

"Right," Susie agreed, slipping the leather harness off the hooks and over her shoulders. Her shoulders bent forward under the weight and her knees buckled, but she managed to stagger back to the cabin, the leather traces dragging on the ground behind her. Her grandmother harnessed up Independence while Susie ran back for the bridles. The two Fjords stood calmly together despite the noise and commotion going on behind them as June harnessed them up. Boomer stood with his head down, his lead line tied to the back of the wagon, too worn-out to care.

Within minutes, the Fjords were hitched to the fully loaded wagon and June shook out the lines.

"Come on, Bella," the girl yelled. "Bring them on down. Old Bossy took care of the rest."

The heifer took one look at the wagon rumbling by with the woman and boy perched on the bench seat, the young girl sitting in the back cradling a calf in her lap, the giant dog laying beside her, and the familiar cow horse tethered to the back of the wagon, and let out a long "moooo". The calf's mother trotted after the wagon, ignoring Bella.

June glanced over her shoulder briefly and started to laugh.

"Why are you laughing, Gram," Billy asked.

"I feel like the Pied Piper," she said.

Susie and Billy looked at the cattle which strung out in a long line behind the wagon, and started to laugh along with their grandmother. For a brief moment, their fears were forgotten.

Chapter Eleven

The Great Escape

    The air was hazy from heat and smoke, the sun but a faded circle in the gray mantle that had settled over the mountain. A sooty layer of ash hung in the air, smothering calves' feeble calls to their mothers and the sound of the horses' hooves on the wagon trail. The world was still, not a feathery gust of wind stirred the trees in the forest nor blew away the dust cloud that encircled the herd.

    The two Fjords jogged down the hill, their eyes weeping and their nostrils clogged with black ashes. The forest fire raged in the upper slopes of the mountain. The animals were jumpy; neck muscles quivered and hair stood on end. The Appaloosa danced nervously behind the wagon, his eyes rolling. All three horses were beset by an uncharacteristic tenseness.

June kept her hands close to the brake, the lines taut in her fists, prepared for the worst. She sensed that any little thing would cause the horses to bolt and the cattle to stampede.

"This is really creepy," Billy muttered, his voice hushed, his eyes roving from one side of the trail to the other.

"Yeah," Susie agreed, turning around to face him. Her legs were half asleep from the weight of the calf in her lap. Its mother stayed close to Boomer, within eyesight of her baby.

"I'm sure we'll run into Andy and the boys pretty soon. They're probably already half way up the mountain," June consoled her grandchildren.

"We've had some bad fires in California over the last few years. The air was like this. The smoke was so thick, it was hard to tell night from day," Susie said. Horse sniffed the calf and licked its face. The calf turned a trusting eye towards the dog. The wolfhound cried and then licked Susie's hand. She stroked the dog's ear, massaging the tips to keep him quiet.

Water bombers rumbled in the sky. They could hear them, but not see them. The horses surged bravely on.

"Easy, boys. Walk," June called out to the Fjords and slipped on a little brake, slowing the wagon's progress.

Billy's eyes got bigger as he hunkered down closer to his grandmother. He didn't want to admit how scared he was, but he was glad he wasn't riding Boomer.

All at once, there was a loud "swoosh". The giant underbelly of a water bomber brushed the tops of the trees. It opened the twin doors in its belly and a cascade of water rushed out. With a loud "splat", the water hit the trees. Limbs bent. Tree trunks shuddered.

Independence

The cattle stampeded.

Boomer screamed and sat back on his haunches, snapping the lead rope.

The Appaloosa darted around the wagon and ran up beside the Fjords, his eyes wide with panic. CD and Independence whinnied and leapt forward.

June slammed on the brake and leaned to the right. The brakes caught. The wagon's wheels locked.

A huge steer barreled past the wagon and slammed into the old Appaloosa's shoulder. Boomer lost his balance and crashed sideways into Independence. Indy toppled. CD screamed as his legs buckled and the two Fjords fell sideways into nothingness.

"Jump!" she screamed to the kids as the wagon skidded down the embankment.

Billy leapt from the wagon and somersaulted across the trail. Cattle dipped and bobbed, their sharp two pronged hooves missing his head by inches as he rolled to a stop. The wolfhound jumped, long legs splaying in every direction. The dog planted itself in front of the young boy and growled menacingly at the cattle. Cattle honked and dodged around the snarling dog.

Susie yelled and gripped the sides of the wagon, unable to move the calf off her legs in time. June threw the lines away and hung on to the bench seat, her head snapping backwards and forwards. Pain seized her back and hips, tearing the breath from her lungs.

Horses screamed in pain. Chains rattled and snapped.

The wagon slid down the hill on its side, blankets, saddles, pillows, and boxes scattering over the steep ground. It came to a screeching halt at the base of a tall Douglas fir tree.

For a moment, everything was still. Dust hung

suspended in the air over the fallen wagon and horses. The cattle were gone.

Billy laid on the ground in the middle of the wagon trail, rolled into a tight ball, arms over his head. The dog stood, head down, sides heaving, golden eyes glowing, in front of the young boy. Susie was sprawled in the earth, her back resting on a tree root, her eyelids flickering. June lay crumbled in what was left of the wagon, her paintings lying in the dirt before her, packages of food and bits of clothing scattered all over the hill.

Indy scrambled to his feet with a huge grunt and a groaning of leather. CD's legs were tangled in harness and leather lines, his breathing short and ragged. Indy looked down at the old horse laying prostate on the ground and lowered his head. His breath brushed the shoulder of the older Fjord, ruffling the fine hairs and lifting up his long mane.

Susie cried. The calf she had been holding had been torn from her arms and now lay at the base of a tree. She thought it was dead until it lifted its head and called out piteously to its mother.

"Grandma," Billy wailed.

Billy peeked over the lip of the embankment and looked down at the fallen horses and the upturned wagon. His grandmother didn't move. Susie was sprawled across the now empty wagon bed.

"Susie!" he hollered down at her.

Susie looked up into the dirty face of her younger brother, at the tears that tracked ugly streaks down his cheeks, and lifted a hand to wave at him. Relief swept over his face.

"Susie, Gram's unconscious and CD can't get up!"

Susie grunted and shifted her hip around. Pain

coursed through her back. She dug herself out from under her grandmother's boxes of paints and reached out a shaky hand to her grandmother.

"Gram?" she asked, her voice trembling.

There was no response.

Susie slid over to her grandmother and lifted her arm, checking for a pulse. She felt a strong throbbing against her index finger. Her grandmother's face was covered in blood from a thin slash across her forehead, but the bleeding was already slowing to a trickle. The old woman's chest rose and fell in a steady rhythm.

"She's okay, Billy. She's unconscious, but she's alive," Susie called to her brother.

"What about CD?" Billy yelled back, wiping the tears from his eyes.

Susie looked at the old horse laying flat on the ground. He hadn't tried to stand up, but she couldn't see any blood or broken legs.

"I think he's alright, but I have to get Gram out of here first," she said. "Slide down the bank. I need your help."

Billy slid down the gravel on his behind. A couple of straggling heifers stopped to peer down at the boy and the dog as they gingerly made their way to the fallen horses and broken wagon.

"What do I do?" he said, his eyes red-rimmed and afraid.

"Help me pull Gram to the side and straighten her legs. I can't find any broken bones," Susie said. "She responds to pressure on her legs so her back isn't broken. At least I don't think it is. We probably shouldn't move her, but we don't have a choice."

"But what about all the blood?" he cried.

"That's just a surface wound. See? It's already stopped

bleeding. I've had worse than that," Susie spoke softly.

June groaned and rolled her head sideways.

"Gram? Gram," Billy shouted.

"Shhh, Billy, take it easy," Susie warned him.

"Grandma," she whispered in her grandmother's ear, "we have to move you. It might hurt some, but I can't leave you hung up in the wagon, it's not safe." June moaned in response and licked the dust from her lips, her eyelids flickering, but not opening.

Susie got to her feet and gripped her grandmother under the arms and tugged. Billy put a hand under one of his sister's and pulled too. With a thud, they managed to haul their grandmother away from the broken bench seat and straighten her body out on the ground.

June grunted and opened her eyes. "Kids?" she croaked.

"Don't try to move, Gram," Susie said. "I'll send Billy for help."

Horse pushed his way in beside June. He rested his head on her shoulder.

"Billy, go find a blanket to cover Gram up with," Susie commanded.

Billy stopped sniffling and ran back up the hill. He snatched an old quilt off the ground, skidded back down the embankment, and then carefully laid the blanket over his grandmother's body. She lifted a hand and brushed his cheek with trembling fingers.

"It's okay, Gram, we'll look after you. I'm gonna go get help," he said bravely.

June smiled, and then winced in pain.

Indy nickered.

"Stay with Grandma while I see to the horses," Susie ordered her little brother. He nodded in agreement.

Independence

Susie made her way over the broken shafts of the wagon. She could see that the axle had snapped in two. It was amazing that they were all still alive.

"Whoa, CD. Easy, Indy," she crooned to the Fjords.

CD lay on the ground, his chest not moving, his legs tangled up in the leather traces and lines. Susie worked her way around him. She placed one hand on his neck and stroked him gently. The Fjord's neck was soaked with sweat and grime. He lifted his head and looked at her. Susie sighed with relief.

Indy snuffled her arm, looking for reassurance.

"Good boy, Indy," she soothed him.

Indy stood quietly licking his lips, his shoulders and haunches scraped raw, but otherwise in pretty good shape. He had a small cut on his right knee, blood caked, but not deep.

Susie slipped between the two horses, all the while talking gently to them, keeping them quiet. She untangled the lines around CD's legs and unfastened the tug chains that were caught between the tree and the center pole. CD grunted, but didn't try to stand up. The inside rein that hooked onto Indy's bit had snapped in two and a piece hung from each of the horses bits. Susie scrabbled back over the Fjord and stroked his face.

"Okay, CD, up you get," she urged him.

The old Fjord scrambled to his feet. He staggered once, caught his balance, and righted himself.

"Good, boy," Susie whispered to him. "What a brave old man you are."

Independence stuck his head under her arm and lifted it upwards. Susie giggled, despite herself, and stroked the felt on the younger Fjord's nose.

She walked back over to Billy and her grandmother.

June's eyes were wide open. Her gray eyes were weepy, but focused. Susie let out a sigh of relief.

A wave of black, greasy smoke drifted down the hill. A roar like wind in a tunnel filled the air.

Billy started to shake.

"Gram, do you think that you can help us get you to your feet? If we can get you up, we can balance you on the wagon and get you mounted on CD," Susie asked. "Billy can climb ride Indy and go for help. The fire's spreading. We can't stay here."

"I think so," June croaked. She gritted her teeth and tried to sit up. With the help of her grandchildren, she finally made it into a sitting position.

"You can do it, Gram, I know you can," Billy whispered to her, his brows knitting together.

June smiled. With all her strength, she pushed herself upwards. On shaky legs, she stood up, Billy gripping her elbow. She nodded at her granddaughter.

"I'll make it. Go get the horses," June croaked, her head swimming as she focused all her willpower on standing up by herself.

Susie twisted CD's line into a tight loop and backed him up to the side of the upturned wagon. "Stand, CD," she commanded. The gelding stood quietly without twitching a muscle.

Billy and Susie helped June step up onto the lip of the upturned wagon. With a lot of pulling and pushing, they flipped her left leg over the horse's back.

June grabbed hold of the top of the wooden hames and held on tight, her face white with pain. Her hips screamed in protest. CD turned his head and looked at her. His eyes were soft, filled with love and trust. June's heart swelled and for a moment, it hurt to breathe, but it wasn't because of the smoke that snaked its way down the embankment either.

"Come on, Billy. I'll give you a leg up. I want you to go and get Andy as soon as I get Gram up to the road," Susie nodded at her brother.

"Okay, sis. You can count on me," Billy said, his mouth setting into a thin line.

"I know I can," Susie said to him, and then cupped her hands below Indy's belly. Indy snorted and lifted his head. He inhaled and honked out a warning. Susie paused, listening. The sound of the forest fire was getting louder. The crackle of the flames gobbling up the trees was now as loud as if she were sitting in the cabin in a chair in front of the woodstove.

"Hurry, Billy."

Billy lifted his foot, slipped his sneaker into her cupped hands, and vaulted onto Independence's back.

"Remember what Andy taught us, Billy, go up the slope sideways, not straight on," she directed him. Billy nodded. "Ready, Grandma?"

June smiled.

Billy picked up Indy's one rein and curled it up like a lariat. Susie had found one of the halters and clipped the lead line onto the inside of the bit for use as a second rein. With the long leather line in one hand and the rope lead line in the other, Billy leaned forward and kicked the horse in the sides, urging him up the embankment.

CD started up the hill after his partner, June clinging to his back. Susie tossed the old blue and white quilt over her grandmother's shoulders, took her place beside CD, and kept a hand on her grandmother's back, supporting her as the horses struggled up the hill. The calf cried out for Susie, staggered to its feet and tried to follow, but its legs weren't strong enough.

The two Fjords dug their hooves deep into the loose gravel, inching their way up the steep slope, and then crested the top of the hill.

"Whoa, CD," Susie said. CD dipped his head into her arms. She gave him a pat, and then turned to her brother and said, "Get going, Billy!"

"Are you sure I shouldn't wait?" he asked.

"No. Go!"

Billy wheeled Independence around and started off at a fast trot, his hands wrapped around the hames, using the two oak pieces of wood for support, his legs sticking straight sideways, the horse's girth too wide for the eight-year-old to handle. Indy pranced down the road, his head and tail elevated, as if he knew he was on a mission. The dog watched him go, his golden eyes gleaming. He whined and panted, unsure if he should follow the boy or not.

Susie stopped and bent over, hands on her knees. Her chest ached. Fire tickled the edges of the trail from whence they came. She hoped that the firefighters would be able to save the cabin, and then laughed. Her grandmother looked at her, her face crinkling into a worried frown.

"I was just hoping that they'd be able to save the cabin," Susie confided to her.

"Let's worry about ourselves first, shall we?" her grandmother croaked.

The two women chuckled.

"I'll be right back," Susie huffed. "I'm not leaving that calf behind now."

June lifted the line and patted CD's neck. He swiveled his haunches and turned to face Susie as she slid down the hill on her buttocks. The wolfhound yelped and whined, still not sure what to do. June reached down and stroked the big dog's back. The dog licked her hand.

Gravel rolled under her sneakers; Susie slipped and fell flat onto her back. The calf let out a terrified bleat. Susie lifted her head and looked at the pathetic little fellow, his curly brown and white coat tinged with black, his liquid eyes filled with fear.

Not ten feet from the calf, a wolf emerged from the brush. Its hair stood to attention and its white chest heaved. Drool dripped from the wolf's curved lips and gathered at the base of its sharp fangs. It uttered a fierce growl, licked its lips, and readied itself to pounce. Its sides were thin, the ribs bulging, its coat matted and unkempt.

Susie recognized the animal immediately. It was the same one that had gone after her on the road.

With a tinge of anger, she realized why the animal was attacking people and livestock. Its left front foot was mangled, crippled by a steel leg hold trap. Andy had told her about the banned traps and how some people still used them. Animals would be left to chew their own leg off, suffering for days. This wolf had somehow gotten away, but was incapable of hunting with its pack and had been driven out. The creature was starving to death.

The wolf leapt for the calf's throat.

A streak of grey lightning blazed by Susie's shoulder as the wolfhound struck the wolf in midair, nailing the frail animal in the rib cage. Both animals tumbled into the undergrowth, rolling over and over. Fur ripped. Teeth snapped. Blood was spilled. A deep growl was followed by a sharp yip of agony.

Susie lifted the calf up and staggered forward. She looked over her shoulder, but the brush was too high. She had lost sight of both the wolf and the wolfhound.

In the blink of an eye, the battle was over and the

wolfhound emerged from the brush, a few strands of white hair sticking out from the corners of his mouth, a crimson puddle of blood coating his pink tongue. The dog licked his lips and wagged his tail.

"Horse," Susie gasped.

Horse limped over to her. There were crimson gashes on his chest. Susie waited for the wolf to stagger out of the bush, but there was no movement. She lowered the calf to the ground and then rubbed the dog behind the ears, knowing that it was for the best, that the wolf was better off dead than living in such misery.

The calf bawled, Susie stood up, and wrapped the tiny thing in her arms. She could feel its heart beating rapidly against her breast. It licked her chin with a raspy tongue. Susie turned and struggled up the hill, the calf's head resting on one shoulder.

"That was close," June stuttered, her face pale beneath the drying blood as Susie crested the embankment.

"Yeah, it was," Susie agreed.

Susie started walking down the trail, her biceps and leg muscles screaming in pain, her grandmother following behind her on the old Fjord. Susie's legs were getting rubbery. She prayed that Billy had reached Andy and that someone was on their way up to help them. She didn't think she was going to be able to go much farther.

"Susie," her grandmother croaked. "I can't stay up here. I can't ride CD anymore, the pain's too great."

Susie bent her knees and lowered the calf to the ground. The wolfhound licked its face and lay down beside the calf, the dog as exhausted as the women.

"Okay, Gram, slide over to the left," Susie said, slipping one arm around her grandmother's waist. "I've got you."

Independence

CD rested his left hind leg, which caused his left hip to drop and his back to lower. June leaned over and a wave of pain shot upwards through her spine. Her vision blurred; the rocks and the trees becoming one. Consciousness slipped away.

"Gram," Susie shouted at her. "Gram!"

Susie threw her right hip forward, catching her grandmother around the chest in a big bear hug before June fell headfirst onto the trail. Susie slid her grandmother carefully to the ground, her own back screaming in protest. She rolled June onto her side and tucked the quilt around her body. June's teeth began to chatter and her body shook with fierce tremors. Susie wrapped her arms around her and held her tight.

The old Fjord nuzzled her arm.

"It's okay, CD, help is coming," Susie stammered.

The Fjord blew on her hair, and then picked up one of the delicate strands in his mouth. Susie reached up and pulled it away from his teeth. The gentle old horse looked down at her, his lips quivering. Susie saw her reflection in his dark brown eyes, her soot covered face, dirty cinnamon colored hair, and faded blue t-shirt with a black surfer stenciled on the breast pocket. The horse pivoted on one foot and began walking away.

"CD! Stop! Come back!"

The old Fjord ignored her calls. He walked on, the sound of his steel horseshoes clip-clopping on the parched roadbed hanging in the air like an off-key wind chime.

The squeal of wheels spinning and gears shifting grew louder and louder. Help was coming!

CD stopped, looked behind him, and then continued on, disappearing into the steadily darkening haze of smoke that now completely blanketed the mountain.

Chapter Twelve

Love's Rhapsody

June sat up in bed, the sun streaming in through the big window creating a bright white halo about her head. She pulled her quilt up to her chest and heaved a deep sigh of regret. Her face was pale and drawn. Thick and unruly gray hair partially covered the tan colored bandage that covered one eyebrow.

Through the window, she could see her two sheep grazing along the far edges of the pasture, the brawny handsome Fjord, Independence, munching along with them. He tipped his large head sideways and bent down on one knee so that he could get at the greener blades beneath the lower fence boards. His Mohawk haircut was long and unkempt. In a couple of days, she'd have to get at it with the clippers to make it look presentable.

June heard her family shuffling around in the kitchen. She hated feeling so helpless. She reached for the glass of water beside the bed, saw that it was empty, and decided it was time to join the land of the living anyway.

June threw back the covers and slipped on her lamb's wool slippers, pulled her nightgown over her shoulders, and picked up the two canes leaning beside the dresser. Her hips throbbed, but the pain was nothing compared to knowing that the cabin and all her paintings had been lost to the forest fire. They were dreadful things, fires. They consumed everything.

June shrugged into her nightgown and made her way out of the bedroom and down the stairs. Her pace was slow, and her back was slightly bent.

"Ah, well, a good cup of tea and I'll be fine. We can always build another cabin," she muttered to herself.

She winced as she stepped down onto the landing.

Melissa saw her limping into the kitchen and ran to take her arm.

"Mum, you're not supposed to be up yet," Melissa chided her gently.

"Can't stay in bed forever," June replied.

Bill pushed his chair away from the table and walked over to give his wife a quick kiss on the cheek. Thomas pulled out a high backed chair for her and Billy ran to get a cushion for it. Andy offered her a steadying hand.

"Here you go, Gram, sit on this," Billy told his grandmother, his red hair falling over his forehead and into his eyes.

"You're in need of a haircut as bad as Indy is, young man," June said, brushing his hair back. "Why don't you go get the clippers from the barn and I'll look after that."

"He's going to grow it out." Susie grinned from over at

the stove. She flipped a couple of eggs over with a spatula. "He wants to be like Sampson."

"He just hasn't found his Delilah yet," Andy asked him.

Billy grinned up at her.

"I'm gonna grow big and strong so I can build you a really big cabin," Billy said, puffing out his chest.

Bill, Andy, Thomas, and Melissa held their breaths.

"A really big cabin, huh? Is that so?" June chuckled.

"This time, it's gonna have two bedrooms!" Billy exclaimed.

"And a bathroom," Susie declared, depositing a plate of eggs and toast in front of June and Andy.

Andy grinned up at her. She smiled back.

"My, that does sound nice," June confessed, raising one eyebrow.

"Susie doesn't want to get bit in the bum by mosquitoes when she has to pee anymore," Billy chirped.

June and the others burst into a fit of laughter. Thomas filled her coffee cup. June took a sip of black coffee, having preferred tea, but who was she to complain. Susie looked positively domestic, standing by the stove with an apron on. Everyone else seemed none the worse for wear.

"You think you can eat both those eggs, Gram?" Billy asked.

"Why? Are you still hungry?"

"Kinda," Billy confessed, eyeballing his sister to see if she was going to smack him or not.

"The boy's got hollow legs and arms," Bill replied.

"And a belly too," Billy agreed.

June spooned one of her eggs onto Billy's plate and picked up a piece of toast. She dipped it into the egg and idly watched the yellow egg yolk spread out over her plate. She twirled the toast in the yolk, but found the thought of eating it made her nauseous.

"What's the matter, June?" Melissa asked.

"Just not hungry, I guess," June confessed. She put down her knife and fork. "What I really want to do is go out and see Indy and CD. I saw Indy in the field, but not a hair of CD."

June noticed that Bill's jaw went rigid. Melissa couldn't meet June's eyes and Susie and Andy exchanged concerned looks. Billy wiggled in his chair. Bill grunted and leaned over the table and picked up his wife's hands.

"Independence is doing just fine. He lost some hair, but it will grow back. The vet says he doesn't think that they'll be any scarring. He's a good horse and has become quite attached to those darned sheep." Bill grinned crookedly. "Boomer made it home safe and sound. Andy's going to bring him over tomorrow."

"Grandma, Andy says I can have Boomer!" Billy chirped. "Is that cool, or what?"

"That's might nice of you, Andy."

"He and Billy are two peas in a pod. Can't separate them now," Andy drawled.

"I want to see CD," June insisted. No one met her gaze. Susie's lower lip trembled as she buttered more toast.

"June," Bill said quietly.

"Bill, CD carried me half way down the mountain."

Bill sighed. Billy threw his arms around her and cried on her shoulder. She gave her grandson a reassuring hug and then slipped out of the chair and grabbed her canes. Horse stretched and rolled off the couch.

"CD's gone, honey. I'm sorry," Bill said even more softly.

"He never came down the mountain," Susie cried. "He

just walked away in the smoke, heading right into the flames."

Andy pushed away from the table, and wrapped an arm around the teary eyed girl. She cried against his shoulder and wrapped her arms around him.

"I'm going upstairs to get dressed, and then I'm coming back down. Bill, please go get the truck. We're going up that mountain," June declared, waving a cane in the direction of the door.

"I'll take you, Mom," Thomas said.

"We'll all go," Bill answered forcefully.

June clumped up the stairs, leaving the family to stare after her.

Within ten minutes, June was dressed and ready to go. Wild horses weren't going to stop her from going up that mountain. She had spent seven days in the hospital and another three at home in bed. She'd had enough of coddling!

Bill pulled the truck up to the front door. Susie, Andy, Thomas and Melissa squeezed into the back seat and buckled up their seatbelts. Billy scooted across the bench seat and settled in beside his grandfather. June dropped the tailgate and the wolfhound jumped into the truck bed.

Indy whinnied at her and galloped across the paddock, his short cut Mohawk bobbing.

"We'll be back in an hour or so, Indy," June called out to the gelding. The Fjord nickered and looked at her, dark eyes keen with interest. "You can't come on this trip."

The Fjord shook his head and thumped a leg against the fence.

"No!" she chastised him, climbing into the Chevy.

"Ready?" Bill asked his wife.

June nodded.

Independence

Bill slipped the truck into gear and they slowly made their way up the mountain.

The ground was parched. A cloud of dust billowed up behind the big red Chevy crew cab. Its tires crunched on the gravel and its springs squeaked and groaned. The leaves of the shrub alders and hawthorns alongside the road were brown and brittle, curling in on themselves. The tall poplars drooped, roots starved for moisture. The forest floor was a carpet of dried needles and dead leaves. There wouldn't be much of a Fall; the heat was killing the vegetation before it had a chance to turn orange or yellow.

The Stetler family traveled in silence.

Half way up the mountain trail, the forest gave way to a patchwork quilt of blackened stumps and partially burned trees. Red fire retardant spattered the roadway. A grimy layer of soot stuck to the truck's sides and coated the windshield with grime.

June saw a filthy mound of fabric at the side of the road and caught a glimpse of small triangle of red and blue squares amidst the seared ruin of her first attempt at quilting. She had made the quilt for Bill to take on the road, a reminder of the family waiting at home.

"Stop here!" she commanded.

"It's farther up, mother," Thomas said, leaning forward.

"I'd like to walk the rest of the way if you all don't mind?" June asked.

"It's a bit of a hike," Bill cautioned.

"That's okay," June responded.

Bill turned off the engine and they all piled out of the truck, knowing enough not to argue with his wife when she got a bee in her bonnet.

Horse whined and jumped out of the back of the truck,

looked around and let out a low woof. Susie scratched behind his ears.

"The air smells like brimstone," Melissa said, wrinkling her nose.

June limped over to what remained of the quilt and lifted it up with her cane. A single tear formed in one eye, but she brushed it away, straightened her back, before starting up the hill.

Bill walked beside her, his eyes roving over his wife's stoic face, ever ready to lend an arm should she falter. Susie and Andy walked hand-in-hand on her other side, Billy beside her, the young boy unusually quiet. Thomas and Melissa walked quietly behind them.

"Have you noticed?" June said, stopping for a moment to rest and catch her breath.

"What's that?" Bill asked.

"The tracks," June pointed with her cane.

Everyone stopped and looked at the dusty trail. There had been no rain. Hundreds of imprints from cloven hooves marred the ground from the passage of the herd of cattle and several smaller herds of deer. Coyote paw prints stretched along the upper side of the roadway. Three sets of horseshoe tracks and one set of Reebok tracks marched down the center of the road.

"Andy, did you pick us up back there?" June waved towards where the quilt was, some hundred yards behind her.

"Yes, ma'am, we did."

"You were in shock. I wrapped you up in the quilt and held you until help came," Susie said, her brows knitting together.

"Billy rode down the mountain on Indy and Boomer had already raced home, am I right?" June asked her

Independence

granddaughter.

"That's right," Susie nodded.

"I didn't have to go very far," Billy added. "Andy and his dad were driving up in their 4X4 and the cowboys were right behind them."

"The boys would have been up sooner, but the cows ran out onto the highway and they had to deal with that first," Andy confirmed.

"What's up, June?" her husband asked.

"Well, look closer at the ground. There are three sets of hoof prints and only one set of human footprints!" June observed. "I'd know Boomer and CD's prints anywhere. Boomer wears bar shoes and CD toes in on the front."

"See, Dad? I told you. You wouldn't believe us," Billy griped. "Me and Susie weren't lying to you."

"That is odd," Thomas agreed. "Although, I never said that you were lying, Billy, just that I found it hard to believe."

"It's downright impossible," Bill stammered, annoyed.

"There is no way that I could have made it this far in the shape that I was in without CD's help and Susie most certainly did *not* carry me," June declared, and then smiled at her granddaughter. Susie grinned back, her expression brightening.

"He was here, Dad," Susie straightened up. "CD did carry Grandma to this point! She couldn't ride him any longer and started to fall off. He walked that way," Susie pointed up the road. "He disappeared into the smoke. A few minutes later Andy and his dad showed up."

"Sounds about right to me," Andy agreed.

Bill stood, hands on his hips, his jaws clenched, his face turning a brilliant shade of red. June sighed and started walking up the hill again, knowing that there was no point in arguing with her husband. The rest of the family followed.

"If that's the case," Bill said stubbornly, "Andy ranch hands would have seen the horse. CD would have had to have run right past them when they checked to make sure that none of the herd got left behind."

"They should have," June agreed, "but they didn't."

"No, sir, they rode all the way up to the lake. They brought two cows down, but they didn't see hide nor hair of old CD," Andy said, tilting his hat back on his head.

"CD would have come home by himself if he could have," Bill added gently.

June wheezed. She stopped and took a deep breath of sulfuric air. Why was it so impossible to believe? Bill was so stubborn sometimes.

"Look up there, Grandpa," Billy wheedled, "you can see our tracks! There's where the wagon went off the road. It was really scary."

"Billy!" Thomas and Melissa exclaimed.

Billy rolled his eyes heavenwards and darted forward. He slid to a stop at the dip where the wagon had clearly gone off the road and looked down the embankment.

"There's nothing left," he howled.

The small group halted beside the young boy and stared down into the abyss.

"Oh, my God," Susie said, her eyes widening. She covered her mouth with her hands, tears welling in her eyes. Instinctively, Andy lifted her hand to his lips and kissed it, trying to comfort her. Susie leaned against him for support. She had done her part, found a strength that she didn't know she had, but was still reeling in the aftershock of the race down the mountain.

June held her breath, her lungs contracting. Bill took

Independence

her hand in his and held it tight.

The gully below was a wasteland. The wagon was a charred skeleton; all that was left were metal axles and circular metal wheel rims. The steel double tree and the chain ends of the tugs were blackened hulks, half-buried in debris. The tall Douglas fir that the calf had fallen against was reduced to eight feet of torched stump. Bits of scorched harness stuck up out of the ground in a series of loops.

Underneath it all were the remains of a white skeleton, its skull mottled with ash, its long nose ending in two sharp points, and its eye's twin vacant holes. One small patch of blond hair was visible on the horse's hind end.

"But he stood up?" Billy said, confused. "That can't be CD! He carried you down the mountain. I helped Susie get you mounted, Gram. That has to be one of Andy's cows!"

Susie tore her gaze away and looked her grandmother straight in the eye. "It is a cow, isn't it? Please tell me that's not him...please tell me that he just hasn't found his way home yet, that's all."

"No, dear," June spoke softly, the tears beginning to fall in earnest. "That's CD. It looks like his neck was broken in the fall. I'm sure it was very fast."

Tears fell from everyone's eyes as they stood in silence, staring at the remains of the old Fjord.

"Gram, you rode a ghost!" Billy whispered.

Birds chirped. They hopped through the burnt out husks of trees, scurried over dead roots, scanning the ground for open seed cones. A light breeze ruffled the earth sending tiny tornados of ash scuttling over the barren ground.

June sighed, and then said to her grandson, "CD gave me the ultimate gift, Billy. He loved me...he loved me beyond all bounds."

June looked at her husband. He squeezed her hand and kissed her cheek. She looked up at the scarred mountain. The sky was a brilliant shade of deep blue and the sun reflected off the rocky peaks. An eagle glided high in the air, above where the cabin used to stand, its wings spread out in all its glory. In the valley below, June knew that life went on, fields were watered, and hay was being cut.

For a moment, June thought she saw a glimmer, the ghostly specter of two Fjords standing at the tip of the trail, staring down at her, bushy black and white manes covering broad necks, their dark eyes gleaming, their coats the color of corn silk. She blinked and the image was gone, but she swore she heard, on the breeze, the sharp jingle of steel on steel, the ping of tug chains swinging, and the gentle creak of leather harness.

Life, by definition,
begins and ends.
Where does it begin?
Where does it end?
Love's rhapsody,
the Light amidst despair!

Appendix: Picture of a basic driving harness

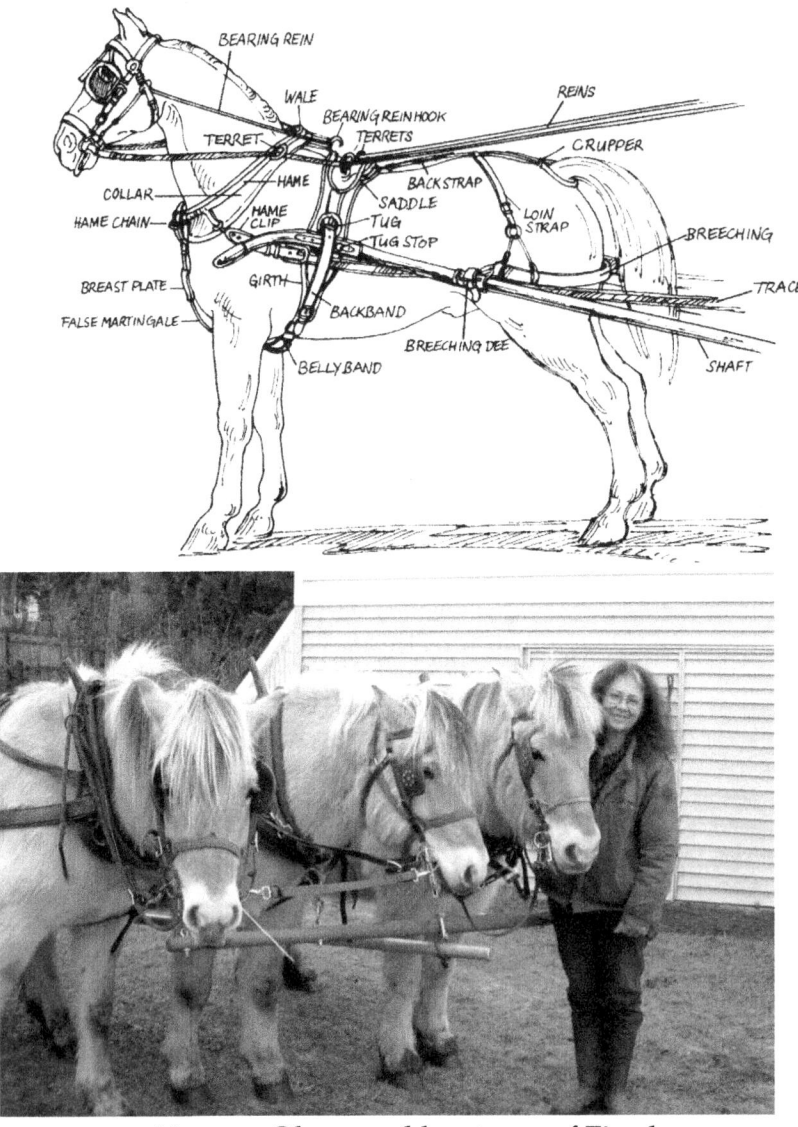

Yvonne Olson and her team of Fjords

Laura Hesse

IF YOU ENJOYED THIS BOOK

All authors depend on word-of-mouth to spread the news about their books. If you enjoyed this book, please consider leaving a review, even if it is only a line or two, on the site on which you purchased the novel.

To receive a free ebook or to receive an automatic email when Laura's next book is released, sign up at www.RunningLProductions.com. Your email address will never be shared and you can unsubscribe at any time.

Valentino

ENJOY THIS PREVIEW

OF

VALENTINO

A blind girl and a Haida boy are stranded on opposite sides of a desolate island in the middle of winter. While the Native boy has a wealth of knowledge and Haida heritage to draw on, the blind girl must rely on her guide dog and an abandoned horse to help her survive.

Inspired by the true story of the horse that got left behind on Jedidiah Island when it was donated to B.C. Parks and a woman who survived for ten days after being shipwrecked on a remote coastline in Haida Gwaii.

Available in print, e-book and audio book.

Valentino
A thrilling story of survival
Laura Hesse

Prologue

The storm that battered the coast also battered the island.

The paint horse huddled wearily beneath the trees, surrounded by a small herd of wild sheep and goats. The animals clung together for warmth. The winter wind drove icy spikes through the horse's shaggy coat and deep into the marrow of its old bones. It was getting harder for him to endure the cold winds anymore and a tired ache had settled into his heart, a deep longing for something that he had forgotten.

The barrel-chested little horse was mostly red with three white socks and a white patch along one side of his body, and a back swayed by age. His eyes were starting to glaze over and it was getting hard for him to see distances anymore.

His eyes roved back and forth beneath his closed eyelids as he dreamed.

He dreamed of a beautiful little girl, one who smelled of apples and spice. He heard the tinkle of her laughter. It was like silver bells on a breeze. His stomach was full and his coat gleamed. He had a warm barn filled with oats and hay and his mother was in the stall next to him.

A loud crash startled him.

He snorted and spooked sideways. Several sheep and goats scampered away from him.

A tree crashed to the ground in the forest on the far side of the meadow. The wind roared through the branches overhead.

He heard something on the wind.

What was it?

Was that a dog's bark?

He wasn't sure.

He turned into the wind. His nostrils flared. He knew that scent. It was the scent of dog, yet it wasn't the time for dogs. Dogs meant humans, but the humans only came when it was warm and sunny, except for The Man of course. The Man brought food, but he never stayed for long.

The horse stepped out from under the tree and followed the dog scent on the wind.

He knew the trails well. He was born on the island and had never lived anywhere else. Even as the forest bucked and buckled all around him, he walked on, heedless of the raging storm. He had to follow the scent.

As he approached the old farmhouse he smelled something else as well. It wasn't apples and spice, but it was close.

The paint broke into a trot.

He trotted past the abandoned farmhouse, down the trail and over the rocks that lead to the sandy spit.

He saw something move in the surf.

He stopped and watched as a big yellow dog dragged a deliciously sweet smelling something out of the sea and up onto the beach.

How unusual.

He snorted and sniffed the air.

Valentino

How marvelous.

It wasn't her, not the 'her' in his dreams, but it was definitely a 'she'.

He walked slowly towards the two beings that glowed like fireflies on a hot summer night, even though they were not fireflies and it was not a hot summer night.

All of a sudden he didn't feel so cold anymore and he knew what he must do.

The old paint horse greeted the dog like an old friend and carefully stepped over the sleeping girl, using his body to protect both the girl and the dog from the stinging fury of the storm.

With a sigh, he closed his eyes against the buffeting winds and dreamed that he was young again, galloping across this beach with a golden haired girl upon his back. For the first time in a long time, he was content and didn't feel alone anymore.

February 13th Sunrise

"Get up, boy," August's father growled, shaking August awake.

"Go away," he muttered and rolled over, pulling a blanket over his head. He wanted to go back to sleep. He wasn't going back to school so what was the urgency?

"Up," August's grandfather commanded.

August uncovered his head. He was greeted by two angry faces: his father and grandfather's. Behind them, dawn was breaking on what looked to be a bleak and drizzly day.

"Grandfather, what are you doing here?"

"You don't go to school, you go to work," the old man glared down at his grandson.

"There are no free rides in this house," his father continued.

"Dress warm."

"Ohhhh," August groaned.

The two men exchanged a sly glance and then grabbed August by the shoulders. They rolled him over and over on the bed until he was cocooned in a wad of blankets. His father grabbed his feet and his grandfather grabbed him under his arms. The two men carried the unruly teen roughly out of the house to the waiting pick-up truck.

"Let me go," August yelled angrily.

The two men threw him into the back seat and then climbed into the front, ignoring his ill tempered outburst.

August struggled to un-wrap the blankets that bound him, but finally managed to do so.

"Where are you taking me?"

The truck careened out of the drive in a hail of gravel.

August stewed in the back seat, his dark brown eyes narrowing. He was angry. What was going on? Why weren't they talking to him?

His grandfather drove, eyes forward, without comment. His father too was stubbornly silent. August grew more and more annoyed by the minute.

The truck pulled out onto the highway, tires squealing on the wet pavement. The trees that bordered the road drooped with moisture. The faint promise of dawn was smothered by a flurry of black clouds which were swooping over the snow topped inland mountains like a World War One Zeppelin war machine.

"There's a bottle of orange juice and an egg sandwich in the cooler to your left," his grandfather told him.

"I suggest you eat it now. You won't have time later," his father advised him.

August stubbornly folded his arms and stared out the window at the approaching dawn.

His stomach growled with hunger. Unable to help himself, he looked at the cooler on the floor. He opened the top and pulled out a sandwich and a bottle of orange juice. He slammed the cooler's lid back down, hoping to make a statement.

"You break it, the cost of a new one will come out of your pay," his father's stern voice boomed in the truck's cab.

August smirked and then devoured half of the egg salad sandwich. It was good. His mother always added sweet pickle relish.

August placed a leg defiantly over the cooler. He noticed there was a bag of clothes and a pair of worn sneakers tucked in beside the cooler. A navy blue sweater with a salmon embroidered on the front was also there. It looked a lot like his.

Wait! That was his sweater. And so were those jeans and sneakers.

And his mother had made him an egg salad sandwich.

She was in on this too?

The truck pulled off the highway and ambled through the streets of Queen Charlotte City on Graham Island in Haida Gwaii. Sleeping Beauty Mountain watched over the residents as they slept. At the harbour, the truck turned into the long term parking.

Several fishing trawlers, seiners, and gill netters were moored together on the docks. The ferry terminal was quiet. A couple of trawlers were already heading out onto the dark waters of the Skidegate Inlet. Lights popped on in the cabins of several others and diesel engines roared into life.

August felt bile rise into his throat.

With a sinking feeling, August knew where he was going.

Maybe school wasn't so lame after all.

Valentino

February 13th Early Afternoon

Maddie was vibrating.

Her world today was a symphony of Technicolor shadows, not black or twitchy like most days. Maddie was legally blind, but could detect some movement within her dimly lit world.

The hand holding her hair brush trembled with each stroke through her long silken hair. The lovable furry face of her best friend, Sammy, grinned back at her pretty reflection in the bathroom mirror.

"Mum says I look like a movie star. What do you think, Sammy, am I a super star?"

The dog barked in agreement.

Maddie let out a laugh, the sound as soft as wind in the willows.

Maddie slipped on the ear pieces to her iPod before reaching for the stack of toothbrushes beside the sink, fingering each one in turn until she found her own. She cranked up the volume to *Style*. She loved Taylor Swift. Taylor was everything that fourteen year-old Maddie dreamed of being.

Maddie brushed her teeth in time to the music. When she was done, she put on her sunglasses and then reached for the handle of the dog's harness.

Maddie danced down the stairs, one hand on the railing, the other holding tightly to the leather handle of the harness that wrapped around her dog's chest and ribcage.

Maddie's excitement was infectious.

The yellow Labrador by her side grinned, tail wind-milling furiously. Drool dripped from the dog's furry whiskers onto the carpet.

Valentine's Day was Maddie's birthday. The day before her birthday was *their* day, hers and her father's. Her father left it to Maddie to choose where and how they would spend their time together. Maddie had woken up that morning knowing exactly what she wanted to do. Rain or shine, she wanted to go out on the boat and feel the wind in her face and taste the salt spray on her lips.

Maddie slid to a stop in front of the kitchen counter. She let go of Sammy.

"Are those blueberry muffins I smell?"

"Yes, but you can only have one," Maddie's mother, Beth, said as she entered the kitchen behind her daughter. Beth wore a pale green nurse's uniform. Her shoulders drooped with exhaustion and her eyes were dark and sunken from having worked a double shift in the ER. A hint of grey touched the auburn hair which was tied back in a dishevelled pony tail at the back of her head.

Maddie pulled the tray of muffins towards her. She broke one in half and stuffed it in her mouth, slipping the rest to the grateful dog.

"Maddie McCracken. Stop feeding Sammy muffins! You know it upsets her stomach and she can't afford to put on anymore weight! Remember what the vet said? Plus you need to keep a couple for later too," Beth lightly scolded her daughter.

"I only gave her half."

"That's a half too much, young lady."

Beth kissed Maddie on the cheek before scooping two muffins out of the tray and wrapping them in a brown paper bag. She placed the muffins inside a blue plastic cooler. Two ham sandwiches, two oranges, two apples, and a neatly packed plastic bag full of dog kibble and milk bones, were already neatly stacked inside.

Sammy let out a low 'wuff'.

"Of course, I wouldn't forget you," Beth said, ruffling the dog's golden fur, and slipping her a milk bone.

"Thought we weren't going to give Sammy any more treats," Maddie mumbled, bursting a blueberry against the back of her teeth with her tongue at the same time. Warm liquid squirted out her lips. She giggled, wiped the purple liquid from her lips with a finger, and then lowered her hand. The dog licked her finger clean.

Beth chuckled and shook her head in exasperation.

"Come on, your father probably has the trailer all hitched up by now."

Beth whisked a silver thermos full of hot tea and the laden cooler off of the table.

"Okay," Maddie responded, slipping a hand around Sammy's neck, and picking up the harness.

Sammy licked her face. Maddie laughed and laughed.

Maddie slowly made her way into the foyer. She sat down and slipped on a pair of hiking boots and a goose down jacket. The dog lay beside her, tail thumping against the wall.

Her mother breezed by them both.

"Don't forget your hat and gloves."

"That's over-kill, don't you think? There's a roof on the boat, Mom."

"Humour me."

"Oh, alright," Maddie said, giving in.

The McCracken family home was a modest two storey Cape Cod house situated on a quiet cul-de-sac in a suburban northwest coastal neighbourhood just outside of White Rock.

An old diesel pick-up truck with a tall fibreglass canopy was parked in the driveway. "McCracken Electric" was stencilled on the side of the truck. Several bumper stickers adorned the new van parked beside it: 'Put the Christ back in Christmas', 'You Can't Fix Stupid', and 'I (heart) Labradors', took up one side of the house. In front of that was a twenty-three foot Campion Explorer boat with the name, *Dawn Treader,* stencilled in black on the bow.

Maddie's father, Joseph, backed the truck up to the boat trailer. He turned off the engine and stepped out of the truck, looking every inch the blue collar electrician from the lived-in work boots to the faded blue down filled jacket and the grease smudged World's Greatest Dad baseball cap.

Joseph McCracken was athletic and wiry. Dark blond hair poked out from beneath his baseball cap, giving him an unruly and untamed look. Steel grey eyes examined the Campion Explorer with practiced ease, the sleek lines of the boat, the coal black stripe, crisp white hull, and 200 horsepower Yamaha motor.

Joseph grinned proudly as he performed a safety check of the boat and trailer, first checking the rigging on the trailer and the trailer lights, before moving on to check the motor and levels in the gas tank on his beloved boat.

Valentino

He ran a hand lovingly over the sleek sides and plush interior.

Before he had time to hitch up the trailer, the front door of the house banged open. He stopped what he was doing and lifted a hand to his mouth to smother a laugh.

His wife was leading the way: a duffel bag bulging with extra clothes for Maddie was slung over one shoulder, an extra blanket for the dog was thrown over the other, a thermos was in one hand, and a lunch box in the other. His daughter trudged along behind her. Maddie's face was a brilliant shade of red, whether from heat or embarrassment, Joseph didn't know.

Maddie was dressed head to foot in a sky blue parka. A fuzzy purple rabbit-eared hat doubled as a scarf. Navy blue hand knit woollen mittens finished off the ensemble. She could barely hold onto the dog's harness. The Labrador's florescent pink life jacket fastened snugly around chest and belly was equally as odd; although, the dog's wagging tail suggested it didn't seem to mind.

"Promise me you'll stay warm. I don't want you coming down with a cold tonight, not with your birthday tomorrow."

"Stop worrying, Mom." Maddie loved her mother, and knew better than to argue, but this was serious over-kill.

"I know, I know, I'm a worry wart. Sue me."

"S'okay, mum. It's just a...."

"Three hour tour," Beth and Maddie sung together.

"That's what I mean. Look what happened to those castaways! I want you prepared," Beth commented dryly.

"Mom, relax!" An exasperated Maddie finished.

"We'll be in the *Dawn Treader*, honey, not an old wooden relic. Maddie's right. Relax, babe, you're just dead on your feet. You've got that crazed, Chicken Little, the-sky-is-falling look," Maddie's father joked.

"A little soap and water wouldn't hurt either," whispered Maddie, wrinkling her nose.

"So now I smell bad? And I rushed home from a double shift to make you blueberry muffins?"

"She's not saying that at all, are you, sweetie?" Joseph said, walking towards his wife and daughter.

"Sorry, Mom, but Sammy and me think a bubble bath is in order," Maddie said, rolling her eyes behind her sunglasses.

Joseph scooped up his wife. He gave her a long, lingering kiss.

"I'm blind, not deaf," Maddie scolded her parents, hot waves of nausea threatening to overwhelm her. The weight and warmth of the parka, hat, and mittens were making her dizzy, and more than a little snappy. "I can hear you necking."

"Get a room," Maddie's seventeen year-old brother yelled as he crashed his way out of the house, hockey gear slamming against the door glass with a bang. Van keys jingled in his free hand. He pressed the remote. The van doors slid open.

Bobbie McCracken was almost as tall as his dad at six foot one. He was as fair haired and fair skinned as his father as well. His sister took after her mother.

"Be careful with your mother's new van, Bobbie. No scratches or ketchup stains, hear me?" Joseph warned his son.

"What about au-de-hockey," Bobbie joked.

"Bobbbieee," his mother warned him.

"I'll be careful."

Valentino

Bobbie tossed his gear into the back of the van, and then popped over to give his mother a hug. He then playfully went to punch his sister on the arm, but she ducked away. The dog barked in fun.

"I'll never figure out how you do that."

"It's easy. You are sooooo predictable," countered Maddie.

Bobbie laughed and ruffled the dog's fur.

"See you later, kiddo. Have fun and don't barf," Bobbie jibed, returning to the van.

"Bro, that's your territory."

Bobbie laughed and waved before getting into the van and slowly backing it out of the driveway.

"I expect you to get at least three goals for me," yelled Maddie.

"If I do, you can have my kitchen duty next week," Bobbie called out the window.

"Not happening," Maddie yelled back.

Her brother gave her one last wave before driving away.

"We better get moving or we won't be going anywhere except around the harbour," Joseph motioned towards the truck. He kissed his wife one more time before liberating her of the bags, blanket, thermos and cooler. He opened the front and back doors of the super cab for Maddie and Sammy and then piled everything on the back seat.

Maddie hopped onto the front seat and the dog jumped into the back, sniffing the cooler with interest.

Maddie immediately peeled off her hat and mittens. She then rolled down the truck's window and fanned her face with her hand.

"Enjoy having the house to yourself, honey. Do like Maddie said and take a bubble bath and get some sleep," he urged his wife as he walked around back of the truck to hook up the trailer.

"So now I look awful and I smell bad," Beth cried.

"Ah, sweetie, I didn't say that," Joseph said, racing back to his wife.

"Oh, yes you did," she cried, hugging her husband, "but you're right, I do stink." She then laughed and rubbed the tears from her eyes. She really was way past exhaustion.

"How far up the coast *are* you going?"

"It's Maddie's call. It's her birthday run."

"Depends on how much I puke," Maddie said, leaning out of the window.

"Maddie McCracken!"

"Love you." Maddie giggled.

In the back seat, Sammy whined happily.

Joseph gave his wife a quick peck on the cheek and jogged around the front of the truck to the driver's side.

"Love you too," Beth crooned.

"Ditto, babe," Joseph replied, before slipping in behind the wheel.

He honked the horn as they pulled out of the yard.

Maddie blew her mother a kiss.

Beth instinctively blew one back.

Beth stood in the lane until the truck and trailer disappeared around the corner at the end of the street. She slowly made her way into the house, shoulders slumping with exhausting.

She locked the door behind her and dragged her feet as she climbed the stairs to the master bedroom.

She stumbled into the bathroom and turned on the hot water. Water gurgled and steamed. Every fibre and muscle in her body hurt. She rubbed the back of her neck, the pain of the long day having inched its way up her spine and into a pounding headache. She sighed and rubbed her temples before returning to the bedroom where she sat down wearily on the edge of the bed.

She fingered the picture on the nightstand beside the bed. The picture was taken in Jasper twelve years ago. Beth and Joseph swung three year-old Maddie into the air. Maddie's hair flew out behind her. She sported a toothy grin. One sneaker was gone. Seven year-old Bobbie laughed at his sister, the laugh so glorious that his eyes watered. Beth smiled, her face glowing. She was so blessed to have such a wonderful family.

Beth headed back into the bathroom, peeling off her clothes along the way. The theme song to Gilligan's Island tumbled through her thoughts. Before long, she began singing it.

Beth stopped singing abruptly, a chill sending shivers up and down her spine. She really was done in. The ER was overloaded and they had lost two people that shift. It didn't matter that she and the doctors and other nurses had done everything they could to save them, or how strong her own faith was, her heart ached for the families who loved those lost souls.

She climbed into the tub and let the hot water ease her tiredness.

As she lay back in the tub, the sound of the empty house enveloped her and she quivered despite the heat from the hot bath.

She groaned and sunk deeper into the water. Still, something dark and ominous haunted her thoughts. She worried about Maddie, too much she knew. Her little girl had endured so much in her short life, the least of which was being born blind and suffering from drop down seizures. God bless her soul, Beth thought, Maddie took everything in stride. Even on the bad days, her sense of humour shone like Olympic gold. Beth wished she had her daughter's strength sometimes.

She took a deep breath, but despite her best attempt at peace, the next verse to the Gilligan's Island song escaped her lips and she shuddered. She prayed it wasn't a bad omen.

End of Preview

Valentino is available around the world on Amazon in print, e-book and audio book.

About the Author

Laura Hesse's educational background includes technical diplomas in Forestry and Geological Engineering. She worked as a Timber Cruiser and Firefighter in Ontario and northern Alberta for ten years and writes about her adventures in the non-fiction novel, *Peter Pan Wears Steel Toes*, as well as draws on some of her experiences as a firefighter inside the pages of *Independence*.

"When an outhouse became a luxury item, I knew it was time to leave forestry," says Hesse. "Now I am inspired by tales of every-day people and animals who wind up in extraordinary circumstances."

Laura lives on Vancouver Island. When she's not writing, you'll find her kayaking or visiting with all of her horsey friends.